D1505378

THE BOOK OF GETTING EVEN

a novel

BENJAMIN TAYLOR

STEERFORTH PRESS

HANOVER, NEW HAMPSHIRE

For information about permission to reproduce
selections from this book, write to:
Steerforth Press L.L.C., 25 Lebanon Street,
Hanover, New Hampshire 03755

Library of Congress Cataloging-in-Publication Data
Taylor, Benjamin
  The book of getting even : a novel / Benjamin Taylor. — 1st ed.
    p. cm.
  ISBN 978-1-58642-143-4 (alk. paper)
  1. Young men — Fiction. 2. Jews — Fiction. 3. Family — Fiction.
  4. Nineteen seventies — Fiction. I. Title.
  PS3570.A92714B66 2008
  813'.54—dc22
                              2008005834

FIRST EDITION

To my brother, in loving memory

CONTENTS

The house next door is never the sanctuary it at first appears to be. If you reach the stage where you are permitted to enter without knocking, you are also expected to come oftener and to penetrate farther and in the end share, along with the permanent inhabitants, the weight of the roof tree.

— WILLIAM MAXWELL, *Time Will Darken It*

PART ONE

THE PURE PRODUCTS

He sneezed four times, always four, like everybody on the maternal side. Sequence was from firm to forcible to fierce to ferocious. Then there'd be peace, in which he felt in his limbs and vitals the secret knowledge of sneezing. Between fits of four the rabbi's son had lived and prospered here — bless you, Babylon, his place to start from, that was New Orleans. One day as a seven-year-old he'd found, on the steps of the temple, a katydid and praying mantis locked obscurely together. Were they killing each other? Falling in love? While his mother watched, Gabriel Geismar had taken a rock from the flower bed and crushed the two creatures, ground them to a uniform paste. She had hauled him up by the shirtfront, she had wept. "For an *experiment*!" he'd protested. She was a deliberate kind of mother, did not say that boys were naughty, said through tears that certain of their deeds were. Feeling good and allied to the violent quick of nature, he'd endured her lecture on unmotivated cruelty.

When she told the rabbi what their son had perpetrated on the congregation steps, Milton Geismar said, with Talmudic certitude, "Little boys live near to the ground. They're in close touch with the insects and like to kill them. All but the tootie frooties do. Make that boy feel guilty and you'll *ruin* him!"

As a father Rabbi Geismar had been demonstrative. Bringing the belt down sharply on Gabriel's butt and bare legs, he'd wailed, in real despair, "*Mamzer!* Curse!" Their only child this was, and not quite right, and the humiliation of it kept Geismar in an active volcanic state, his violence the deep-down magma ready on a pretext to leap up. A son should not cling to his mother. A son should not be so afraid of things, reptiles, firecrackers, unfamiliar odors. There was, in addition, Gabriel's fear of vomiting — other people vomiting. (When the rebbitzin would drop him at the picture show on Sunday afternoons, she'd go in and ask the management, since he was too shy, "Is there any vomiting in this picture? Because my boy can't take it.") A son should not be such an eccentric prig. A son should not have bathroom secrets. A son should not draw filthy, dirty, disgusting pictures for his mother to find under a desk blotter or at the back of a drawer and break down over.

These Gabriel somehow couldn't keep himself from producing, year after year. When he was nearly fifteen, his father had crooked a finger and confronted him with one of the more original — a man embracing a member that grew Sequoia-like from the middle of him and disappeared into the clouds — and sent the boy flying with a slap. A watershed slap, as it turned out, the last of its kind. Something in Gabriel's stare as he got up from the floor, holding his cheek, must have frightened Geismar. Something said: *You are a brute and a fiend and I'll never resemble you in any way or grieve when you go. You are as unhappy an accident in my life as I am in yours.* A stare can say a lot. *Each of us is the other's misfortune, shake hands and a bargain. But if ever you try to hit me again . . .*

That spring Mrs. Kilbourne, in charge of literature at New Orleans Country Day, had presented twelfth grade with *The Rime of the Ancient Mariner*. "In his loneliness and fixedness," she told them, like she'd just thought it up, "the Mariner yearneth towards the journeying Moon, and the stars that still sojourn, yet still move onward." She was an actress, when pedagogy demanded. She closed the book and finished from memory: "And every where the blue sky belongs to them, and is their appointed rest, and their native country and their own natural homes, which they enter unannounced, as lords that are certainly expected and yet there is a silent joy at their arrival." Kilbourne knocked the senioritis out of them with that. All minds bent to her.

She told about the *acte gratuit* — espoused by a café philosophy of recent prestige. But Gabriel felt he'd got there long ago and without any help from Romanticism or the Existentialists. Without, moreover, any of the Mariner's inconveniences. Bless the creepy crawlers of the earth, bless them unawares? There'd be no lurking, sadder but wiser, at wedding feasts, no seeking for someone to confide his guilty secret to. In the long ago, without a pang, Gabriel annihilated two bright green things.

Having skipped third and sixth grades along the way, he won, at sixteen, a full ride to a college he liked the name of, even if considered hard to say by friends and relations. Came the third week of August now, 1970, time to go. To get public facts out of the way: the previous week Janis Joplin had flown home to Port Arthur for her tenth high-school reunion. On Block Island twelve FBI agents posing as bird-watchers nabbed Father Daniel Berrigan, a fugitive from justice since his conviction on charges of destroying Selective Service documents. By the banks of the Pedernales, former President and Mrs. Lyndon Johnson enjoyed a private screening of *Patton*, the hit movie of the summer. In San Francisco, Beniamino Bufano, who fifty-three years earlier had protested America's entry into the Great War by severing his trigger finger and sending it to Woodrow Wilson, died in penury. At Tan Son Nhut airfield, Spiro Agnew would praise the South Vietnamese for "suffering so much in freedom's cause," pledge "no lessening" of American support, and add that "the Cambodian situation seems to be developing very well."

Meanwhile, in New Orleans, Dr. Sheldon Kretschmar, pediatrician, booster, the worst, the noisiest Nixon-lover in town, pillar of the American Medical Association, who'd seen Gabriel through chicken pox, scarlet fever, mumps, and, in early adolescence, a spell of asthma so severe it had led to pneumonia, looked down the youth's throat one last time and said, "Tulane or LSU?"

Neither. Gabriel named the college of his choice as best he could with a depressor on his tongue. Dr. Kretschmar took it out. "Swarthmore," the rabbi's son repeated. He'd put off this checkup to the very last day, but couldn't matriculate without it.

Kretschmar revolved the name. "Never heard of it."

"Swarthmore College, sir, outside of Philadelphia, and a good-looking place by the brochure they send."

"Well, I've never heard —"

"It's a liberal arts college." But the word "liberal" in all its meanings seemed to trouble Kretschmar. He looked Gabriel up and down, seeing not less than another Rosenberg or Hiss in the making, and wished him all the best.

After any doctor's appointment, even with the optician or the orthopedist, when Gabriel came home the rabbi would ask, "Did he look down your throat? Did he look up your address?" — which as a little boy Gabriel had thought funny; but for how many years can you laugh at the same joke?

"Dad, *please*! You've been saying that since I don't know when."

"Nonsense, son, I just now thought it up!" Milton Geismar, like fathers generally, rehearsed all quips till they stood there embodied and part of the furniture. You are beaten, you are entertained. You don't know from one quarter-hour to the next what kind of day it is. Conundrum of Gabriel's young life: In addition to being a trollish and savage father, Geismar was a game and witty one. Any pulpit humorist can say to his congregants, "How odd of God to choose the Jews." But it takes inspiration to add, "Not odd of God. The *goyim* annoy Him." (He was a preening father, too, propelled by unconditional self-admiration. They'd told Milt Geismar he looked like Victor Mature. It went to his head.) At home, by some counterstroke of temperament, regular as clockwork, the charmer would vanish and there the hellhound ogre would be, soberly telling wife and child that they had ruined his life. "Both mentally and physically! I will get a breakdown, do you hear?" Then his voice would drop to an urgent, confidential register. "A *nervous* breakdown." Mother. Father. Because of her you knew you were cherished. Because of him you knew you were in harm's way. Gabriel had reason to regard the story of Abraham binding Isaac as nothing remarkable. A father was somebody who might decide to kill you. He'd carry on in third person, like a sports hero or gangster: "Tell a lie to Milton Geismar? You'll wish you *hadn't!*" "What Milt Geismar says he'll do, he *does!*" Bragging on himself, threatening you: "*Nobody* double-crosses Geismar!" Or else he'd start to blubber and need comforting. Nervous breakdowns — what exactly did they look like? The rabbi's son had settled on an image, not displeasing, of the old man doing violence to himself — tearing off his ears, ripping loose his lower jaw, plucking out his handsome eyeballs.

That evening Gabriel took a valedictory ride to town on the St. Charles Avenue streetcar, got off where the track turns around at Poydras, walked along Chartres, then briskly down Toulouse, looking for an infamous low green door in the wall. A gentleman in a public facility at the levee had told him this was the place. You paid your money, you went in, you had yourself some fun.

He stripped to nothing at the locker provided, then thought better of it and, to restrain the bare fact, pulled his shorts back on, for this hideaway excited at once with its miscellany of smells, an omnium gatherum, musky, civety, Liederkranzy, of what a celebrated periodical of the day only boasted of being but these baths were: man at his best. (Told that that magazine was for "the man's man" and utterly misunderstanding the phrase, Gabriel had hurried off to buy a copy. Any mention of the word "man" stirred him. Even a copy of Reinhold Niebuhr's *Nature and Destiny of Man,* found one afternoon on his father's highest shelf, had merited fifteen seconds of browsing.)

He entered the warren of cubicles, moving briskly through corridors of men with towels around their middles. Each open door framed in the variable light a bare male, some recumbent on cots, some standing; some showing off. As for the closed doors, they were also very interesting. Gabriel had an impulse to knock at one, hearing mirthful noise from inside, but thought better of it.

Farther down the hallway a grinning king-sized cracker tossed his head side to side, saying as Gabriel passed, "Git in here, sugar," beckoning with an authoritative motion of the arm, assured, official even, as if directing traffic in an emergency.

Which this was. Gabriel entered. Expertly, the man kicked the door shut with his foot. He asked in the courtliest way if he could take Gabriel's underwear off. This is what they mean by "den of iniquity," Gabriel told himself. I like it. But twelve seconds later, having moaned and shuddered back into his real and habitual self, awakened from the pleasure, he felt another way entirely and pushed the head aside, yanked up his underpants, and wanted to be out of there. His mind veered to numbers, clean things, cleanest anywhere in or out of the world. Primes, the haughtily exclusive category of those divisible only by themselves. And perfects, perfect on account of being equal to the sum of their divisors. And amicables, two numbers each of which is equal to the sum of all the exact divisors of the other except the number itself. On these it was a particular pleasure to dwell. 220 and 284 for instance. Gabriel added the divisors, just to confirm their amicability ($1 + 2 + 4 + 71 + 142$, like that), then those of 284 ($1 + 2 + 4 + 5 + 10 + 11 + 20 + 22 + 44 + 55 + 110$). Easy in your head. But now try 17,296 and 18,416. Some four hundred such pairs of amicable numbers have been discovered, with more out there certainly. But whether the number of them is finite or infinite nobody has yet nailed down; Gabriel would give his eyeteeth to know.

Here was where he returned to, the frontier he reconnoitered: infinity. The physical universe may or may not be a case of it. But the mind, as attested by calculation of any irrational number to the nth decimal place, plainly was. And this was the real fun, according to Gabriel, embodied passion being but the other fun. Now the worshipper on the floor, exultant in his degradation, kissed Gabriel's hand, his poor put-upon left one, then drew back, asked the inevitable question. "What's wrong witch yuh hand?"

"Born that way." The standard answer he gave.

"Don't make no diffunce."

But it had, it did. For such an irregularity little allowance is made. At intervals you must be reminded. The littlest thing, really, an error of some kind in the genetic manufacture of him — on his left hand Gabriel had two thumbs, absolutely identical, down to the moons in the nail beds and the lines across the knuckles. Conjoined Siamese-style, functioning perfectly well as one, they had yet drawn the stares and incredulity of the world (of New Orleans, that is) and made for Gabriel Geismar a destiny.

"Looks like when yuh see a turnip or tomatah trying to turn into two." And now the man bestowed a kiss specifically on the thumbs. "What's yuh name?"

No answer.

"What's yuh name?"

"Um, Forrest, Forrest Delavoy," Gabriel lied, pressing into service the name of a detested classmate at Country Day.

"Forrest Dee-la-voy! I do like that name."

Here Gabriel made to leave, shaking the man's hand, businesslike; but the irony of it caused a laugh to well up in both of them.

"Don't say goodnight."

"I've got to go somewhere tomorrow morning."

"Where you goin'?"

"Pennsylvania."

"Pensuh*vain*yuh? You college boy?"

"I am."

"Knew it even witch yuh clothes off! How come you go way up there?"

A shrug. "I've got to head home now."

"You ain't even asked my name."

No, indeed. Gabriel had wanted this man nameless as a cloud or clump of earth.

"Clarence Rappley. I ain't from here. Wouldn't be from here on a bet. I'm from Dulac. Not Dulac itself. Outside of."

"Good to know you," Gabriel said, and saying so seemed to scatter his resistance a little. Clarence helped himself to a kiss, and though Gabriel intended it to be closemouthed and brief, that kiss lingered out, opened up, tasted good.

"Let's go back to my crib."

"Down in *Dulac*?"

"Outside of."

"No."

"Yuh place?"

His place, excellent, with a rabbi and rebbitzin asleep down the hall. "No, Clarence."

"Just lemme walk you home."

Getting loose of Clarence Rappley would not be so easy as saying no. "All right, then."

"Go put yuh clothes on."

———

They walked up Toulouse, then down Bourbon, not saying much, drawing only an occasional stare from the milling, gabbing, falling-down throng — Texans, Arkansans, tourists out for a big time, some of them by that hour relaxing in the gutter. These revelers were busy, didn't care what a big hayseed and a little Jew were doing on the town.

At the edge of the Quarter, Gabriel again tried to take his leave. "So happens I be goin' yuh way," Clarence Rappley told him. "What street yuh live on?"

"Josephine," Gabriel lied.

"I just happen to be going to Josephine myself."

So at St. Charles and Poydras they boarded the streetcar, in which people did stare. Clarence outfaced them. "Nice night if it don't rain!" He took the seat beside Gabriel and threw a companionate arm around him. "Stop it!" Gabriel growled. A gentleman in a seersucker suit and white shoes and a boater looked interested. A freckle-faced colored woman fixed an eye on Gabriel's supernumerary thumb. A marmish blond woman made a small mouth and looked askance. A pitch-black man in a busboy's uniform said, concurring, "*If* it don't rain." Gabriel leapt up, made for the other side of the car. "I don't even know this person! He's followed me all the way from Toulo— I mean from Chartres Street. He's ha*rass*ing me!"

"Call the po-lice, you so upset," suggested the freckle-faced woman, and let out a laugh.

The seersuckered man, who'd been screening himself with the day's *Picayune,* kept peering over it. "Like she say, call the law!" the busboy said, and let out a hoot. Everyone went silent, waiting for the other shoe to fall, which it did. A loutish drunken character was emboldened to yell, as those two blacks were the only two on board, "You jigaboos shut up!" Astonished silence. "Bad enough having to ride with you." Silence, shame. "And you there, you pipe down too. Don't know him — in a pig's ass you don't!"

With that the seersuckered gent disappeared altogether behind his *Picayune*. Gabriel pulled the cord, quickstepped from the car at Lee Circle. Head lowered, bullish, Clarence Rappley followed.

Gabriel flew down Howard, Clarence hollering after him the plain truth. "You cahwud! Cahwud's what you is, Fahrust Delavoy! If that's even yuh name! Cause it sounds mighty *phony* to me!" Storming on, not turning around, Gabriel noticed he couldn't see the pavement for tears starting into his eyes, couldn't have spoken if he'd tried, but turned now to face his rightful accuser. Clarence slapped at the air, then made as if to punch Gabriel, right left right, but careful that the blows fell short, and was upon him in an ironbound hug. Gabriel wriggled a moment. Clarence Rappley set him free.

Like an uncupped bird he flew now, veering for home, there to put all real events behind him. He took out his mathematical diary, put down a few random things that had occurred to him that day — two or three indeed having germinated even as he ran the rest of the way up St. Charles, then down Terpsichore. Ah, now for calculability, sweet detachment from the corporeal universe and its demands; here in the abstract manipulation of symbols of quantity according to unchangeable rules was the freest of feelings. Integers, fractions, reals, imaginaries, transcendentals. Bliss. He'd have a little equational fun — oh, paradise of getting even — outside the boundaries of three-dimensional space, while the heavens churned around him, while in other galaxies, worlds beyond us, other minds behold in who knows how many dimensions. Beyond us, though not utterly — we can with symbols exploit these dimensions by all orders of magnitude. Before bed Gabriel puts himself through his non-euclidean paces. Equations lengthen out on the diary page. A falcon with the hood still on, he calculates in his darkness. And how is it, he wonders, that whatever is matter or energy is numerical? Whence this unstinting *effectiveness* of numbers? The answer is so deeply hidden that this our average solar system may well expire, its star out of fuel, before our species or some post-anthropic intelligence of the earthspeck finds out. The why of it may forever be too hard, the way arithmetic is too hard for earthworms. But of the how of it he'd make himself master.

Now he opened the window screen, hung himself out, and swung around for a look at the Milky Way, grindstone of stars; gaze out from earth along the plane of the disc and you see the thousands of millions of them, the vast smear of light, vaguely bifurcated — our neck of the woods. At thirteen, the rabbi's son had entered a stationer's shop on Calliope, plunked down his money, and ordered a supply of engraved letterhead reading GABRIEL GEISMAR, COSMOLOGIST. That is to say, historian of the physical universe. He knew what was his to do.

The night freshened. He finished packing, brushed his teeth, climbed into bed. New Orleans outside his window had settled down. He recalled for the first time in more than an hour that he had three thumbs instead of two. And at the instant of nodding off heard a voice say, "What's wrong witch yuh hand?" and "Don't make no diffunce." Now all the Gabriels, on such timid terms with one another by day, broke the bread of sleep. A covey of bobwhites settled on the rabbinical back lawn. Picked and nattered, *bob-WHITE, poor-bob-WHITE.* Went away.

———

How fine the manicured suburbs of Philadelphia smelled by comparison, the sticky-coned firs, the fresh-cut grass, the wormy windfalls, the berries baking. He who'd never till now crossed the Mason-Dixon Line marveled that here crickets sang from midafternoon; that the air was crisp and piney and immaculate, not murky and laden. No ordinary campus, the Swarthmore grounds were officially an arboretum: cedars, spruces, maples, lichen-spotted oaks (one of them three hundred years old), even a few carefully maintained elms. There were a rose garden, a peony garden, and a pinetum. Catalpa, crepe myrtle, buckthorn. And an amphitheater with cedars standing amidst the granite tiers. But the glory of the place, Gabriel saw at once, was a gorge, the Crum, edged with joe-pye weed, black-eyed Susans, devil's paintbrush.

Hot Tuna roared from an improvised public address system on the green. An unofficial banner garlanding the doorway to Parrish Hall announced THE PURE PRODUCTS OF AMERICA GO CRAZY. (Those in authority had let it stay, keeping their powder dry for bigger infractions.)

Gabriel skipped out of the official orientation. He knew which way east was. While he unpacked, a scent of patchouli came through the open door, followed by a pale and silent figure. Wearily, she seated herself on the bed.

"Stooges," she said.

"Beg pardon."

"Stooges and running dogs."

"Who?"

"Nearly all of them. My name is Mireya." She rolled the *r* prettily.

"I'm busy now."

She smirked. "I like a man who knows enough not to go to orientation." She stood up, inclined to him.

He nudged her back. "The loverboys'll be back before long. A wide array to pick from."

"A wide array of stooges."

"Also running dogs. One's right for you." Who was this distinctive-smelling girl? Evelyn Mitskie from Shaker Heights, who'd taken "Mireya" as her nom de guerre and carried the banner for billions who were voiceless.

"Are you telling me to leave?"

"I'm wrong for you."

"Why?"

"Reasons. Trust me."

"Come to my room for a minute. I've got something to show you."

"Do I want to see?"

"Something precious. From far away. From the other side of the world. Something . . ."

Get her back to her room, he reasoned, then get rid of her. He followed.

"I've decorated already," Mireya told him. The door to her room was festooned with the moondoggie of the day, Dr. Guevara. Inside, the walls bristled with mottoes from Lenin, Ho, Fidel, Frantz Fanon, Herbert Marcuse, Eldridge Cleaver, Bernardine Dorhn.

"I can't stay." It stank in there of cigarettes and patchouli and what all. She produced from a dresser drawer her treasure, extended it reverently in one hand: *The Little Red Book*. She said all one needed to know was in it. Nattered on about Mao as if he were a close personal friend — Mao this and Mao that.

Gabriel was edging out.

"We know there are enemies of the people among us," she seethed now, "even here in this pastoral sanctuary, which is no sanctuary at all, which is run from the top down to suit the capitalist criminals who own it. Why *wouldn't* they monitor those speaking here for the wretched of the earth? Why *wouldn't* they plant spies among us?" On and on, a suburban Joan of Arc got out in camouflage. (So as to be what, Gabriel wondered — less visible on campus?)

"Enemies like who?"

"Like . . . *you!*"

Eighteen hours in a new place and already he had an accuser. But not he alone. Mireya had selected several whipping boys right away from the Sun Belt states. Down the hall was a nice kid from Dallas who'd pasted President Kennedy's inaugural address to his door and decorated the walls inside with photos of the Kennedys, all of them, even Joe and Rose, even Eunice and Jean, even Peter

Lawford. He had plenty of books by Arthur Schlesinger Jr. and John Kenneth Galbraith and was, at the moment this dragoness of the New Left passed, reading *Profiles in Courage*. It brought out the prosecutor in Mireya. "Love me — *love me* — LOVE ME — *I'M A LIB-ER-AL!*" Worse than Birchers, worse than Klansmen, worse than Nazis were liberals.

Another on her list of enemies of the people was a girl from Coral Gables with scarves and hosiery and a Utrillo poster, who planned to major in French, minor in art history, and take her junior year at Grenoble. Poor thing was guilty of conspiratorial crimes the minute Evelyn Mitskie's eye fell on her.

At dinner, served from five to six, Gabriel put down his tray at an empty table. Almost immediately, a couple sat down beside and across from him. Who were these besiegers? The girl introduced herself as Marghie. "It's Marghie with the *g* hard." "I'm Danny," her companion said. She was light-boned and rosy, arresting to look at, with a head of hair red and auburn and sun-bleached at the crown. Helplessly she'd push it behind her ears, only to have the paler locks fall forward. She'd push it back. Her hair kept her busy. On her wrist was a man's watch, an outsize, battered Longines. Danny was something else again, olive-skinned and black-eyed, a type of Oriental prince in glasses. Set amid his perfect teeth was a sickly incisor that made him vulnerable-looking when he smiled, which he continuously did, even when chewing.

What were they? Maybe lovers. But Gabriel sensed, running between the two, a more fundamental complicity.

"Freshman?' Marghie asked.

Gabriel nodded.

"We're seniors," Danny said.

Marghie said, "He and I started out together," and tipped her head Danny's way. "Started out together," he echoed, and tipped his head back at her. And now, Gabriel saw it clear as Danny told him, "We're twins."

"Twins," she echoed.

"One of nature's merry tricks," Danny said.

"She played it on us," Marghie said.

Everybody knows some — has a set in the family or goes to school with them or just stares at a pair in the street. You can't get through life without this mystery of two instead of one presenting itself, this confounding of identities. An emptiness opens beside you. You wonder, where's my twin? Gabriel said, "I went all through school with these identical twins and they —"

"Identical twins are of no interest," Danny informed him flatly, with suddenly no smile at all.

"None," Marghie confirmed.

So that's how it was. But it occurred to Gabriel that fraternals might secretly envy identicals, for the greater glamour was unquestionably theirs. It's identicals who make strangers gawk and smile, expecting to be smiled back at on the curious assumption that, because they look confoundingly alike, identicals must themselves be amused by the fact. When what they're surely thinking is, Why can't people leave us alone?

"How many sets of identical twins in Shakespeare?" Marghie asked. "Zip. How many fraternals?"

Danny answered, "Shakespeare's lousy with them. Shakespeare's got —"

"One set, to be precise," Gabriel said, Shakespeare being his single enthusiasm in the so-called humanities, which he regarded by and large as a refuge for squishy minds. The real humanities were mathematics, physics, chemistry, and biology, in that order.

Marghie reached under the heavy mane to give her neck air. "Are you sure?"

"Very," Gabriel said. "And by the way, there is in Shakespeare what must be a set of identicals — in *Comedy of Errors*. Unless Antipholus of Ephesus and Antipholus of Syracuse are identical the plot doesn't work."

"Go to the head of the class," Marghie said, "and tell us, while you're there, what that funny accent is."

"This is, I guess, the New Orleans accent. While we're on the subject, what's that funny accent you two have?"

"We come from Chicago," said Danny. "But have no accent."

"Like fun you don't."

"Tell us more about *Comedy of Errors*," implored Marghie. "We were riveted."

"It just happens to be something I wrote a paper on last year. At New Orleans Country Day."

"Where you paid attention," said Danny. Was he making fun? What was so bad about having paid attention? Evidently the jaded talk of seniors, wishing now to conceal the studiousness that had brought them this far. Their table manners were atrocious. Had wolves raised them? They certainly made no mention of any parent. But then neither did Gabriel, come to think of it, or anybody else. Such was the pleasure of being there: make-believing you owed nothing to those middle-aged, middle-class, two-bit players who called themselves your mom and dad. Parents were the very last topic to suggest itself. Wolves had raised the whole student body and that was that.

Gabriel observed that these northern people had a way of priding themselves unduly on their opinions. Ordinary conversation could escalate into stridency, stridency into taunts and jeers. Conversation in New Orleans wasn't like that. You conversed in order to agree. Failure to agree threatened the social fabric. Either there was agreement or there was a change of subject. (Even Jewish conversations had this quality, in New Orleans.) But what did these northern showoffs really *know?* How a combustion engine works? Or a television? Why airplanes don't fall out of the sky (except occasionally)? Gabriel had taken apart and reassembled a short-wave radio when he was eleven. Rabbi Geismar, unable to contain his pride, sermonizing in the quasi-British tones rabbis of the Reform persuasion are prone to, had worked this marvel in one Friday evening. Gabriel went on at fourteen to win the Louisiana State Science Fair, held at Baton Rouge. He'd suspended drops of oil to measure the charge of a single electron. Two years later he put a metal plate into a vacuum tube and connected it to the negative terminal of an electric battery, demonstrating by a luminosity produced at the end of the tube the presence of cathode rays, controlled emission of which produces the television images Gabriel's contemporaries stared at for six hours a day. It puzzled him that ordinary people have so little curiosity about the way nature works. Still less about the way their conveniences work. A mirror, a ballpoint pen, a jukebox, a fire extinguisher. Never mind television, pneumatic hammers, hovercraft, electrophotography, data processing, atomic clocks. The only way, Gabriel knew, to be at home in the world was to understand these things one and all, to make friends with nature and to make friends with technology, which is the harnessing of nature for human purposes. This was what he knew, so far.

Danny had begun to dilate on his favorite philosophy course of last year, "The Search for Values."

"Did you find 'em?" Gabriel asked, smiling away, betraying more than a little contempt. Shakespeare was one thing, but all this insufferable *philosophizing* was a waste of time. He hadn't left his father's house to hear again about "values," a favorite word of Geismar's in the pulpit and at the dinner table. Gabriel held to Galileo's view — that he'd rather discover a single fact, even a small one, than debate the great issues at length without discovering anything at all. He wanted nothing to do with those sickening, superstitious monuments to wishful thinking, those comprehensive value systems, the world's great religions, deploring them as loose abuse of language, futility, a coming out by the door wherein you went; three generations of rabbis had brought about their opposite in him. Quite apart from the tribal claims to a special relationship to the (of course nonexistent) godhead, what appalled Gabriel was the mind-numbing ritual *repetitiveness* of Judaism — the going in circles like a jackass around a millstone — in this respect no different from the futile empty round of other faiths.

For "faith" Gabriel Geismar had substituted "finding out." Better a single fact, even a small one . . . And yet an odd residue of the piety of the fathers went on declaring itself in him: He could not bear the thought of bivalves, would as soon eat a June bug as an oyster. Of the ramified and venerable structure of Jewish law and practice, this fragmentary prohibition was all that remained.

"Did I *find* them? Certainly not," Danny told him. "The search — the *search* — is everything. Philosophy's the love not the possession of wisdom. *PHILO-sophia*." And this was admittedly a good answer, even if in saying it Danny sounded like the dummy in some professor's lap. Well, he *was,* but winsome, bright, Charlie McCarthy not Mortimer Snerd.

Gabriel said, "Don't you want to find out new things, instead of just thinking again what people thought a long time ago?" That was science talking, all-conquering science.

"There's the trouble with you types," Danny said, "wedded to a myth of progress, pledged to a Faustian bargain."

Marghie's blue stare, moving between them, settled now on her brother. " 'Faustian bargain' — you got that from Dad."

"I did *not*!" Danny said, and gave her — it was hard to believe such practices held sway at the senior level — a noogie on the upper arm. "I got nothing from that old fart!" She noogied him back, and all was well again. But what, Gabriel wondered, *about* their father? At last someone had made mention of a parent, only to be shushed up.

Later that night he went to an on-campus screening of *I Am Curious (Yellow)*. Audience reverential. (Movie no good.) And who should be running the projector but Marghie. It was her film series, getting off to a woeful start. Some of the upcoming features sounded more promising, however: *Children of Paradise, The Seventh Seal, Zero for Conduct, Boudu Saved from Drowning, Lola Montès, Potemkin, Diary of a Country Priest, The Bicycle Thief.* Plus *The Lady Eve, Notorious, The Apartment, Touch of Evil.* Plus *Kind Hearts and Coronets, The Third Man, The Astonished Heart.* Plus *Tokyo Story* and *Ikiru.* Plus Marghie's full-scale retrospective of the works of Carl Theodore Dreyer.

Back at the dorm, nobody wanted to sleep. Candy McHugh, a freshman in hip-huggers over a leotard, skinny as Olive Oyl, told Gabriel that the Veil of Maya must be lifted. What? He hadn't heard about it? A beaky, dry-as-dust senior, Sam Zwerling, talked nonstop about his upcoming honors topic, politics in the poetry of Dryden. Craig Pearlstein, a spotty, heavyset freshman from Norfolk, Virginia — and Gabriel's roommate, alas — grew quiet. The psilocybin he'd eaten was taking hold. Gabriel left Pearlstein prone, mute, and fanatically examining one corner of his blanket.

Three doors down Natalie Greenspan, a ferret-eyed sophomore with amusing hair and a breakneck delivery, seemed already to know six or eight languages and hogged the oxygen and was the McCoy, no doubt, but so original was the idiom that no one knew what she was saying. Gabriel grasped that the two of them would get along fine. But the resident assistant, that persnickety Muriel Binstock, was another matter. This bleak girl derived from the South Dakota Black Hills. Evidently there were Jews even there. One needn't go now in search of them. Here was an exemplar, stamping her foot from day one.

Much later that night, his first out from under the home roof, Gabriel decided he liked all these new neighbors, even the baleful Binstock and the ludicrous Mitskie. He liked a girl from Morristown, New Jersey, who had mastery of the *I Ching* and wouldn't stop playing her Buffy Sainte-Marie album. (It was now four forty-five in the morning.) He liked a boy from Poplar Bluff, Missouri, who liked Buffalo Springfield and had the longest hair of anybody at Swarthmore and a poster of Neil Armstrong on the moon with "BIG DEAL!" blazoned beneath the image. He liked whoever the deep thinker was four doors away who liked the Moody Blues. He liked a girl from Phoenix who preferred French to English and whose every second sentence involved the phrase *"mon amie Muriel de Chicago,"* a good chunk of the French she actually knew. He liked a boy from Lake Forest who adjusted his groin a lot and whose strained and tearful look indicated not homesickness but contact lenses he was having a hard time with. He liked a girl from Santa Monica, a delicate Korean beauty who kept to her room and played soprano recorder. He liked a boy from Chesapeake Bay who'd waited tables the previous summer at Annabel's Fish Camp and wore a T-shirt with the restaurant's slogan — *We've got the crabs!* — on both sides. He liked a crunchy granola from Burlington, Vermont, who wore a Mexican wedding shirt, listened to bluegrass, and was intriguingly hairy. He liked a girl from Newport News who broke wind freely and whose candor was backed by ideology: the personal as political, the liberating return to nature. (If she's nature, give me artifice, thought Gabriel.) He liked even messy old Craig Pearlstein, insensate on the bed opposite. What the hell, he liked them all, for while people here talked about nearly everything, they said not a word about his surplus thumb, nor even seemed to notice. This place was all right.

No Che Guevara on the wall for Gabriel Geismar. No Mao. No Angela. Instead he'd hung up, on his side of the room, a little engraving of Carl Friedrich Gauss, his current hero, who at nineteen figured out how to construct a seventeen-sided polygon using only a compass and straightedge, who at twenty-two discovered non-euclidean geometries (but kept them a secret), whose ten years of research in geodesy produced most of the fundamental discoveries for differential geometry, probability theory, statistics, and surface theory. The history of mathematics knows many great ones but just three absolute peaks. Archimedes, Newton, Gauss. (But why not Archimedes, Newton, Gauss, Geismar? It sounded good, sounded plausible.) Archimedes had used ever smaller polygons to measure circumference . . . Newton had used ever smaller units of time and distance to measure instantaneous speed . . . Gauss had plotted the results of survey readings to show that the resulting graph has the shape of a bell, thereby establishing his law of the distribution of errors, shaveable to an ever smaller margin . . . Lesson of the masters from Zeno of Elea onward: ever tinier differences between ever tinier intervals, infinite divisibility, the glory of numbers. And in the quick of such infinitesimals was where the beauty and the truth lay. Between any two fractions there must be infinitely more fractions, as between any two points on a line infinitely more points. Something familiar as the sway of a tree limb in the breeze, or the flight of a bird to a sill, or the leap of semen onto his belly and chest, required for its full analysis quantities that, while larger than zero, are vanishingly small. Only infinitesimal calculus can cope with the various unfoldings, in generation and decay, of this exhaustively quantifiable real world. And granted a real world as interesting as that, and still too young to have noticed that he was generation and decay too, Gabriel Geismar believed it would be a folly and a shame ever to die.

––––––

"My Very Earnest Mother Just Served Us Nine Pears" binds to memory Mercury, Venus, Earth, Mars, Jupiter, Saturn, Uranus,

Neptune, Pluto. On that model certain mnemonic devices for stops along the Media-Elwyn Line were proposed en route from Swarthmore to Thirtieth Street Station. "Idiot systems" Danny and Marghie called them. Stations were — Angora, Fernwood, Landsdown, Gladstone, Clifton, Primos, Secane, Morton, Swarthmore. Gabriel came up for starters with "Awful Floods Left Geese Cackling Pitiful Sorrows Mid Sunrise."

"Not bad," Marghie admitted, and frowned.

Now was Danny's turn. "Alms From Local Groups Could Provide So Much Solace."

"How dreary," said Marghie. "How *drab*! You sound like some old biddy with that."

"Does it fit or doesn't it?" he demanded.

"It fits all right, like a *drab* little orthopedic shoe!" Now she proposed "A Fine Looking Girl Can Provoke So Many Scenes." (Indeed. She was provoking one right now. People had started to turn around.)

Gabriel burst out laughing with a good one, "A Fat Lazy Guy, Craig Pearlstein, Suddenly Moved South," and wished it were so.

"After France Licked Germany . . ." Danny began but could get no farther.

"After Fear Left Gabriel . . ." Marghie tried, but this too hung unfinished.

"After Fear Left Gabriel," Gabriel said, "Cold Perseverance Showed Mighty . . ." but he couldn't figure out the rest without resorting to nonsense, which was against the rules.

They had a half hour's wait at Thirtieth Street Station. It was the last week of November, the first snows flew, and the glass walls at both ends let in a shadowless light. The waiting room had perhaps two dozen pigeons flying through its upper reaches, alighting above the electronic board or along the lintel that ran around the room or between the rows of wooden benches jacketed in marble, then taking again to the air, all in a day's work.

Gabriel had been fretting about a split seam in his backpack. "I've heard it said, Marg, that a girl always has a safety pin somewhere on her person. Any truth to that?" She produced one after a search.

Most memorable at Thirtieth Street was a bronze monument to the dead of 1941–45. A male angel, wings arched above him, bears a fallen soldier to heaven. And around the base, a little scene of cruelty played itself out. A boy of junior-high-school age attempting to tag along with six or so of his peers was being roundly rejected, pushed to the floor at last. Marghie saw the tears well in his eyes as he got up and brushed himself off. "I'd like to go over there and give those sons of bitches a piece of my mind."

One thing to say it, but that's just what she crossed the great hall and did — went over to those bad boys and, hands on her hips, said something that caused them to step back together like a frightened herd. Then she turned to the tagalong and said something to him, put a hand on his shoulder. "Wherever Sis is is her kingdom," Danny said, watching her. "Act right or off with your head."

"I bet things like that just didn't happen at the Lab School," Gabriel said when she got back. Of late, he'd turned loose his idealizing tendencies on the Laboratory School, where Marghie and Danny had gone from kindergarten through twelfth.

She gave him a look. "Gabe, we at the Lab School just sat there having Platonic dialogues. *Of course things like that happened!* I saw enough meanness just in the girls' restroom to last me. You cannot believe what monsters some of the popular ones were. I remember there was this pimply loner, Rachel Wickstrom, who hadn't been seen for a week, and those popular witches went around saying Rachel had died of acne."

"There was Paula Schwartz," Danny put in, "who was a nice person. They called her Polish Warts. Laughed their popular butts off about it."

"I remember one time in the lunchroom at Country Day," Gabriel said. "Forrest Delavoy and his pack of apes came up to this skinny, limp-wristed guy who ate by himself and Forrest stuck out his jaw, you know, like Mussolini, and said, for everybody to hear, 'We were just wondering, Kenny, are you a boy or a girl?' Well, of course, the camp followers of those guys began to giggle and say 'Oh, Forrest, you're so funny!' and like that, but then Kenny stood up and said, 'Am I a boy or a girl? *Both*, you idiots! Can't you see I'm *both*?' That did for Forrest and his assholes. It was something. Then Kenny turned and smiled at me. Not that we were friends. The bond was more like between galley slaves. We were serving the same sentence. He knew I'd come in for my share of torment." Gabriel raised the Siamese thumbs. "*This* was not let off lightly . . . Forrest and his goons were so bored, so raunchy, so stupid that in study hall, to upset the girls, and Kenny and me, they'd take out matches and set fire to their flatulence."

"That we did not have at the Lab School," Danny said. "Unfortunately."

The train to New York was crowded. Marghie and Danny dashed for the last two seats. Gabriel stood a while. Danny opened the book he was reading, *The Long Loneliness,* by Dorothy Day. Marghie kept urging Gabriel to sit in her lap, which eventually he did. She straightened the part in his hair, gave him a peck behind the ear, told him what a good boy he was. All this made him a little sleepy, so he put his head on her shoulder and shut his eyes. When he opened them he saw Danny in profile, one seat away, sleeping with his mouth open, *The Long Loneliness* face down on his chest. Gabriel studied the brow ridge, the trace line of fuzz where the razor had stopped, the peevish lips, the mound in the throat.

They swayed pleasantly, sleepily together. Marghie dozed and waked. Then something got into her. She struck up a campfire tune. *"As I was walking down the street a billboard met my eye."* She gave her brother a little poke in the ribs. *"The advertisements pasted there would make you laugh and cry."* Sleepy-eyed, Danny stretched and smiled in recognition. *"The wind and rain the night before had torn those signs away, and what was left upon it did make the billboard say —"* Here her brother, evidently a veteran of the same campfire, joined in, two tones lower. *"Go smoke a Coca-cola! Drink catsup cigarettes! See Lillian Russell wrestle with a box of oysterettes!"* Their voices rose. More people turned around. *"The pork and beans will meet all right and have a finish fight! Hear Chauncey Depew lecture on Sapolio tonight!"* These references were paleolithic. Who the hell was Chauncey Depew? What was Sapolio? Who was Lillian Russell? All evidently the carefree humor of an age ago when the century was young and blithe, not old and mean.

And speaking of mean: the conductor now came by to admonish Danny and Marghie — and Gabriel too, even though he wasn't singing. No more monkeyshines or he'd put them off the train at the next stop. Marghie shot him a curl-up-and-die look and finished hotly in Gabriel's ear, *"Bay rum is good for horses! We have the best in town! Castoria cures the measles if you pay five dollars down!"* as Danny pounded out a tattoo on the upholstery. *"Teeth extracted without pain for the cost of half a dime! Overcoats are selling now a little out of time!"*

———

"Are you related to Gregor Hundert?" Gabriel had asked as soon as they said their last name. He'd put the question more or less jokingly, not having met anyone related to a famous person and assuming the people he could meet were from an obscurity similar to his own.

From Danny no flicker of pride for a Nobel Prize–winning relation. "He's our father," he'd glumly said. Hundert, a name spoken in the same breath with Bohr and Szilard, Rabi and Bethe, Teller and Fermi, Oppenheimer and Lawrence, Ulam and

Feynman, a wizard like them of the cloven atom and its awful might. Professor and Mrs. Hundert had come that week from Chicago to New York, he to give a lecture at Columbia, she on a research errand to the ethnographical division of the Public Library. They were stopping at the Gotham, dignified and modest across Fifth Avenue from its costlier cousin, the St. Regis. They'd arranged communicating rooms for the twins on a different floor from their own. Marghie had called ahead to say she and Danny would be bringing a friend who could share Danny's room.

Because they were seniors, Danny and Marghie had single dorm rooms. In hers, one evening last week, she and Gabriel were having silent study hall, as they called it, theoretically no talking allowed. But they couldn't help swapping comments, each opaque to the other, on their respective readings, his in superconductivity, hers in Siegfried Kracauer's theory of film. It was much more fun to study together. After ten minutes of scholarly silence, Gabriel had said, "Remember about what Kenny said that day? About how he was a boy and a girl both? Well, what would you think if I told you that I'm not all boy?"

Marghie looked up slowly from her Kracauer. "I'd think you were underestimating me."

For just a minute or two, Gabriel explained, or for a day or two, without warning, when going to sleep or walking into town or raising his hand in class to answer a question, he'd feel like a girl. Yes, he did appreciate the anatomical disparities, knew as well as anyone that the species is divided into male and female. But such categorical certitudes seemed to him, in the shifting light of his own experience, oversimplified. He'd not told anyone about this before Marghie, who said not to worry, that occasionally, just for a minute or two, or for a day or two, she'd feel like a boy.

Then the phone had rung and he'd picked it up and said, "Marghie's room." A middle-European voice, feminine and fond and readily warm to the unknown boy at the other end, said, "Yes, please, may I speak with Margaret?" Gabriel had paused, charmed to silence, and so the voice added, "If she is available."

"One moment, please." He pulled a face, handed Marghie the receiver. What she commenced to speak was a glossolalia interspersed with shards of English. It sounded like no language at all. It was ghastly, an idiom played backward. It was Hungarian. *"Édesaniám, nagyon szeretlek,"* Marghie finally had said, and hung up the phone. And this was the same girl who could swear at you in American with the vitality of a Marine, gain the upper hand always with her native profanatory gifts, alongside of which powers lay another kingdom of words, back of the armoire or through the looking glass, and there she and Danny went to play without you, speaking the unassailable tongue of the Magyars.

They were doing it now, on the train — some by-play of mutual recrimination, apparently about Danny's having overpacked, as always. "If we let you, you'd pack the toaster." Plunging into darkness at Weehawken, the train came to rest some minutes later in the deeps of Penn Station. Up they bounded through the beastly place. First thing Gabriel's eye lit upon was a couple of nuns, smoking under their coronets. He hadn't known they were allowed. An old fantasy reasserted itself — to go up to a nun, fall to his knees and say, "Sister, I am lost!"

He told Marghie, who said, "I'll give you fifty bucks if you will."

"Would have a minute ago, but I'm out of the mood."

That year, in New York City, schizophrenia had stepped out of the shadows and into the limelight. Gabriel saw a florid woman pacing around in front of the Long Island Railroad ticket windows. Her mouth opened and closed in tardive motion. She wore on her head a medley of things — a birdcage, a stuffed monkey with a blood-red mouth, some drapes, a plaster bust of JFK, a hot-pink bolster, a toy ironing board, a snowfall in a glass dome, a fitted sheet, a model B-52 — held in place with a bedspread and fastened under her chin with a clasp. This headdress was half again as tall as she was, and she wore a feed-bag dress and, over it, a hand-painted sandwich board that said on either side,

PLEASE EXCUSE
MY APPEARANCE.
I AM FORCED
TO CARRY
HITLER'S
DIRTY LAUNDRY.

"What are we supposed to make of that?" Danny said.

"Poor thing," Marghie said.

Gabriel said nothing, because the sight filled him with horror and made his stomach hurt. You didn't see the likes of her in New Orleans, not even in the depraved reaches of the Quarter above Dauphine Street. They walked all the way from Penn Station to the Gotham. Professor and Mrs. Hundert, who'd already retired and would rise early, had left a note at the front desk: "You young people enjoy yourselves, and we will see you tomorrow." This in Mrs. Hundert's hand. She gave an address where they would meet at noon for lunch, a club to which the professor belonged. To this sepulchral place Marghie and Danny had been brought over the years whenever the family visited from Chicago. "Please remember to dress properly," she'd added in a postscript.

Marghie exhaled with drama and handed the letter to Danny. "Tuckered out," she said, and went to her room. Danny and Gabriel decided on a walk, a timid one up Fifth and west along Central Park South. They stopped at Prexy's for a late snack, hamburgers with the special Prexy sauce. They looked in at Rumpelmeyer's, a kind of ladies' tea room decorated with stuffed animals. They got as far as Columbus Circle, then retraced their steps. The New York Athletic Club, the Essex House, the Hampshire House, the St. Moritz, the Navarro, the Barbizon Plaza, Prexy's, the Plaza. And opposite lay the great park of parks, pathways dimly lit to reveal — this amazed the Chicagoan and the New Orleanean alike — people strolling around without a care for their lives. Could it be, Gabriel and Danny wondered, that locals had simply not heard about the oblivion awaiting them in there?

They had a look in the F.A.O. Schwarz windows. "I had one of those," Danny said, pointing to the electric train circulating in the store. "Smaller than that, without the bridges and tunnels."

"Marghie didn't have one?"

"Still doesn't." Howls. "Never will." Howls in the night.

Back at the hotel, they climbed in their beds and turned out the light. Exhausted but restless, Danny kept up a desultory line of talk. "What's the worst thing that ever happened to you?" he asked into the darkness. He had, like his sister, a knack for the shortest cuts to intimacy.

"It didn't happen to me," Gabriel started in. "It happened to my cousins in Lake Charles, and to my grandmother, and my aunt. Nine years ago. House caught fire in the night. It was the first cold snap. Uncle Nahum had fixed the furnace earlier that year. He was a do-it-yourself guy, whether he knew what he was doing or not. When the furnace came on the house went up."

"They all died?"

"Some of them. My three cousins. They hid under their beds and suffocated. And my grandmother. Aunt Tannie survived, but so damaged she doesn't know her name, or that she ever had children. Just flops around in bed, or lies quietly. A nurse lives in. I've only been to see her once, only I didn't. I stayed in the next room. I heard the noises she made."

"What about your uncle?"

"Unhurt. He'd corralled everybody on a sleeping porch, but my cousins ran back to their rooms. Their cat Molly had had a litter a month or so before. I was there visiting when the kittens were born. I think the girls must have gone back to look for Molly and her babies. A wall of fire came up through the floor. It cut them off. My aunt and my grandmother tried to go through to them. They must have called for help. They hid from the fire under their beds, and that's where the firemen found them. Not burned at all. They found Molly too, and her babies, alive, just a little scorched on their fur. She'd taken them one by one, at the first smell of smoke, out a dormer and across the roof and down to a rain gutter over the garage. And there they stayed, meowing under an eave."

"How'd your uncle hold up afterward?"

"Can you imagine, knowing a little mistake of yours had done all that? I couldn't stand even to think about him. One little mistake and you're, you're —"

"Carrying Hitler's laundry."

"He didn't need to put on a sign saying so. He did other things. Spread out on a park bench the next day and ate ice cream for everybody to see. Dripping down his shirt, he didn't care. People said, 'Nahum, get hold of yourself!' He snuck off to the *movies* the day after the funerals."

"And after that?"

"He just got very quiet."

"And after that?"

"A bowel tumor ate him alive." Gabriel snapped his fingers in the dark. "I think he'd grown it from shame . . . At first I thought my father would cry permanently. Really, I thought he'd keep crying. Then he stopped. The subject was just never mentioned again. His view seemed to be that the dead ought to be treated as if they'd never existed. I said so to him and he threw an ashtray at me. Not at my head, but it hurt."

"Mom and Dad talk very quietly in German sometimes. All very calm, I've eavesdropped. Marg too. We can't make out what they say though. It's not about us. It doesn't seem to be about them either. I think it's things that happened before we were born."

A silence widened out now, as if their beds stood on opposite banks of a river, and a traffic of barges and tugboats halted by, and the stars came out daintily, and the deep current pulled, and all at once there were no families, only them. "Would you come over here?" Danny said. "I think you should come over here."

Which like an arrow Gabriel did, landing more or less in the middle of Danny who took Gabriel's head in both hands. "Now you're with me . . . Now you're with me."

———

A squat, sooty structure of Beaux Arts persuasion, glowered over by skyscrapers, the club held its charms in reserve. On the second floor were two airy rooms with a foyer between them: to the left, a library with red- and green-leather sofas and chairs and a table piled with periodicals; to the right, a room wallpapered in pressed leather, with bukharas underfoot and subfusc pictures on the walls, examining one of which were Lilo and Gregor Hundert.

He turned first, a big man through the middle, wearing suspenders that held his pants chest-high; a nutcracker face — apple cheeks, eyes alight under snowy brows, nose a puggish fixture, mouth whiskered and drawn down in a catfish way. Everything about him, down to the cherrywood stick he carried and the way he tucked his necktie into his trousers, told of a time decades ago. Yet radiating from Hundert, it seemed to Gabriel, was an energy foursquare in the world and determined to last.

Mrs. Hundert appeared young enough to be his daughter, a lean woman, handsome without vanity, weathered around her pale eyes, hair swept back from a face open and expectant as she turned now.

"Hi Mom," Danny said. Mrs. Hundert kissed him two times, then a third. Fists buried in the pockets of her cardigan, Marghie allowed herself to be kissed too, then gave the professor a hug. "Hello Dad," Danny said, hanging back a little, till his father forced the issue with a quick embrace.

"And this will be Gabriel," said Professor Hundert, turning on him a quick glance. "Wery pleased." Gabriel felt the familiar mix of shyness and impulsiveness percolate through him. He was seconds away, he knew it, from tripping over a rug or walking into a jamb or saying the disastrous opposite of what he should.

"We are so glad to meet you, Gabriel," Mrs. Hundert said, warmly taking him by the hand. Like the professor, she said the *a* short and put emphasis on the last syllable, turning him slightly, pleasantly, into somebody else. Gabriel could feel himself gaining composure, finding a stance. She was helping him, sealing already the compact between them, this woman he had known for seconds. She was respite and swift nearness and what he suddenly, unreasonably wanted was to lay an unquiet head on her shoulder. He felt himself falling and standing still and felt himself struck, for this other kind of love is as prompt as lightning too.

"Come, children, lunch is upstairs," the professor said. His accent was much heavier than Mrs. Hundert's, and as Gabriel would have imagined it out of his meager frame of Central European reference: He sounded like a vampire. Gabriel kept telling himself, *Gregor Hundert, Gregor Hundert.* He'd been to the Swarthmore library to do a little research. There were *books* on the shelf about this man, one of the so-called Hungarian Eight, a more potent cluster of scientific genius than has hailed from any other place and time, ever: Theodore von Kármán, George de Hevesy, Michael Polanyi, Leó Szilárd, Eugene Wigner, John von Neumann, Edward Teller, and Gregor Hundert — "the Budapest miracle."

Today was certainly the first time Gabriel Geismar had wrung history by the hand. A series of mathematical marks on chalkboards had brought about the new era, the long peace, the Pax Americana — surrogate wars abounding but great-power war, world war, spoiled now, made unfeasible. And here climbing the red-carpeted stairs alongside Gabriel was one of its sovereign makers.

"Did you and Mrs. Hundert have a good flight?"

"Sewere snowfall in Chicago."

In lieu of a good social instinct prompting the logical next question, some inner devilment drove Gabriel fifty questions onward. Having no talent for small talk, he leapt now to the large: "Was it coincidence all eight of you were Jewish?" The old man only kept climbing, seemed not to have heard. Oh, mistake, mistake! But when they reached the dining room, and had seated themselves, and put their napkins in their laps, and sipped their ice water, Hundert turned and said,

"No."

Gabriel had spoken earnestly to the rock, and now the rock poured forth. "The insularity of Budapest was harrowing for young men such as myself. The only intelligentsia there *was* there was Jewish. But God help you if you were so identified, in as much as ewidences of a fertile mind were the mark of Cain in that atmosphere."

(How did he decide when to say the *v*'s like *w*'s? He didn't always.)

"Jewish by chance? No, no — inewitably Jewish. And in a dangerous situation, at least by my time. The day before I turned eleven Horthy rode into Budapest on a white horse and threw out the communist government — Kun and the rest, many of them Jews, who had lasted one hundred thirty-three days and done great harm with their Hungarian Socialist Republic, you should pardon the expression. And then was the price to pay. Although just a little boy, I got acquainted with the most terrible thing in human affairs, which is collective retribution. Only a foretaste of the unimaginable things to come."

The devilment that had got into Gabriel was growing. He hazarded the very question he wouldn't have dreamed of putting: "Did you know Edward Teller back then?" He was playing dumb, of course, as the clever young are apt to, knew perfectly well that Hundert and Teller, exact contemporaries, had attended secondary school together in Budapest. Knew also that after Teller's famous betrayal of J. Robert Oppenheimer in 1954, and Oppenheimer's consequent loss of security clearance, Hundert had refused all contact with his oldest friend.

"Know Edward Teller? Oh, I could be said to know him. In Budapest, let me see, his father was a lawyer, and they lived in a pretty house on the Pest side. And my father owned a tannery, and we lived in Buda. Pest and Buda, two cities conjoined — you understand about this. Edward was my classmate at the Minta, which was a better school than such a place had any right to. Many Jewish administrators and teachers were on staff there at the outset. But by the time Edward and I arrived — these were the early years of Horthy — the faculty was a mix of those older ones alongside a new breed, young revanchists who poisoned the schoolroom. I wividly remember a teacher addressing his classes as 'Gentlemen, Jews, and Polacks.' With a smile, of course. How one learned to fear that sort of smile."

Breathing shallowly, shifting in his chair, Danny looked like he might break for the door.

"As for Teller, we were quite close, really, in those years. He was a wonderful young man, dogged, ungainly, but with a ravishing mind. Also highly musical, did you know? And a demon at chess."

The professor looked dreamily across the room, as if communing with old Budapest, then shot up an arm for their waiter.

"I lost contact with him for a bit, during his time at Munich and mine at Göttingen, and when a few years later we found ourselves studying together again, this time in Leipzig under Heisenberg, it came as a great shock to see the misfortune that had befallen Edward. Ewidently, in Munich he'd leapt from the platform of a moving streetcar and fallen, causing a foot to be severed. And what walor he showed, for which we loved him. For which Heisenberg in particular loved him. It surprises people nowadays when I say so, of course, but in those years my hero was Edward Teller . . . He was a lovely fellow."

Noise of ice in tumblers, silverware against china, loud all at once.

"He came to the States in, I think, thirty-six, the year after I arrived at Chicago. We would see each other at conferences. And then we saw each other again, daily, we two boys from Buda and Pest, in the Jemez Mountains of a place called *New* Mexico — we hadn't known there was a new one — and this is the part of the story that you perhaps know. Los Alamos, where we worked together for more than three years. Certainly the strangest time of all our lives. You have been to this part of the world, Gabriel?"

"No, sir."

"Oppie chose it. He'd been there as far back as the early twenties, I think. He knew the mesas and canyons like the back of his hand. They had passed their summers there, you see, he and his brother. Privileged, brilliant, aesthetical boys. Riwerside Drive boys. Their father built a business in order that his sons should one day be not businessmen but scholars. Oppie remembered one mesa in particular and this was how we came to be at Los Alamos. The altitude of the place impaired my judgment, and not mine alone, leaving me and others of the theoretical diwision to wonder if we had furnished sound calculations. Some feared the gadget would fizzle. Fermi, on the other hand, joked that it would ignite the nitrogen in the air and the hydrogen in the oceans and put paid to the planet. He would grin and give you the odds, as he figured them, on such an outcome. Oh, I liked and admired Enrico, but did not share his sangfroid. I truly did wonder if we were drunk on the mountain air and plotting the incineration of the uniwerse. Better a *tausendjähriges Reich* than that, I told myself in the night."

A phantomlike waiter brought menus.

"I lost weight. A mortal fear of snakes preyed on me. Teller came to my room with a diagnosis. Homesickness. But for where? Chicago? Certainly not. Leipzig? I cannot tell you how I hated the thought of Germany and all things German. Budapest? No. Edward got a metaphysical brainstorm. He said I was homesick for somewhere I hadn't yet been." Here Hundert seemed to drift a little, then came back. "I have always admired very much Mici, Teller's little wife. She is most appealing."

Danny and Gabriel ordered club sandwiches. Marghie, a dedicated vegetarian opposed even to dairy, got the mixed greens. ("Sucker," Danny said, as always when she placed her veganistic order.) The professor got a Gruyère and Parmesan omelette, Mrs. Hundert steak tartare with a coddled egg on it.

"Teller connived to ruin an innocent man, one of the greatest the United States has ever known," she said, "then feigned not to have wanted the result he deliberately brought about. An honest villainy would have been preferable. As for the lovely young man who was Edward Teller, I suspect a closer look would reveal capacities for betrayal that were in him always." Was a domestic quarrel about to break out? (Gabriel had never seen his own mother contradict his father. Once every few years she'd shriek. Habitually, though, she communicated only through the repertory of somatic protest: ulcers, anemia, facial neuralgias, tachycardia, stones everywhere.)

"No one admired Oppie more than I, my dear. I only think Edward's case more complicated than you do." He turned again to Gabriel. "Tell me, young man, what do you know about Robert Oppenheimer?"

"Only his work on general relativity before the war. And the charges against him later on."

"Yes. This work on relativity would ewentually have resulted in a Nobel Prize, had he lived long enough. Forecasts, in effect, the existence of black holes, does it not? He was the supremely mysterious man of our lives. Translated — but perhaps you know this — from the *Gita* in his spare time. Kept a little pink-colored Sanskrit edition always near to hand. A couple of nights before the test at Alamogordo, he spoke for me some lines of it he'd put into English. 'In battle, in forest,' . . . I seem not to be able to remember. I admired it so much that I asked him to write the werses down, which he did, and we memorized it," he said, appealing now to his wife.

A slow smile lighted her. "In battle, in forest," she said, "at the precipice of the mountains, on the dark great sea, in the midst of javelins and arrows, in sleep, in confusion, in the depths of shame, the good deeds a man has done defend him."

They had a moment to look at each other before Danny jumped in: "You talk about the good Oppenheimer and the bad Teller, this great difference between them. I think it's small change. I've read Dorothy Day and she says the real distinction is between those who lend themselves to killing and those who don't."

Marghie exhaled heavily and examined the ceiling. Coloring up, the old man said, "There was no choice but to dewelop and use that weapon, Daniel. Would half a million more American casualties in 1945, and millions more of Japanese, have been preferable to the action taken? This is what an inwasion of the home islands would have involved. We dropped those bombs and ended promptly the war of subjugation Japan had begun, barbaric and genocidal throughout China, Korea, Indo-China, the Philippines, Borneo, Malaya, wherever they went. We bombed cities from the air because that's what they had done, because that was the city-destroying war that they, like their German allies, had decreed. And in the end we used a weapon fantastically greater than any they possessed to end the horror that they, not we, had unleashed. It worked, and left each of us who participated to his conscience. Mine tells me that what we accomplished was not just scientifically inevitable but morally correct, and that what the president decided to do with our product was correct also."

Marghie propped her chin on her fist and smiled a little smile. "Harry Truman never goes out of style at our house," she told Gabriel.

Mrs. Hundert said, "That will do, Margaret."

"That, *that* will do? It's the first thing I've said today." She glared with indignation at her mother's steak tartare.

"Why wasn't the bomb demonstrated in an unpopulated place?" Danny said. "Why on Hiroshima? Why on Nagasaki?"

"Factions favoring and opposing surrender each had the emperor's ear. It was necessary to make the point in no uncertain terms in order to compel an end to the losses on both sides. A clinical demonstration of the fission bomb would not have sufficed. I am not at all certain that Hiroshima alone would have sufficed."

"Oh, reasons why! The whole war machine has its reasons why!" Danny sat up straight. *"Criminals, then and now!"* He tossed the hair from his eyes. "I'm a pacifist today, and would have been one back then."

"Wery high-minded, my boy, but tell me, just for the sake of rigor, that you honestly feel the Germans and the Japanese should have been handed what they wanted, which was, between them, the world. Tell me that your pacifism extends to giving whole continents away to the tyrants who happen to want them."

"Some of us must speak for the highest moral standard, which renounces violence under all circumstances."

"And some of us," his father replied, "must cope with human nature as it is, rather than dreaming of human nature as it ought to be. Do you think this weapon was an outcome of physics any of us would have hoped for, ideally? But the force of history pushed physics that way. We did not know if the Nazis would be able to produce such a thing themselves. They had in their employ a number of wery considerable physicists. And they had fissionable material. Uncertainty about the state of their atomic program was the compelling urgency. The thought of Goering's Luftwaffe in possession of a uranium bomb caused the midnight oil to burn on the mesa. These were the worldly facts, Daniel. I find them more persuasive than your unanchored platitudes."

They'd arrived, father and son, at their usual impasse. The dessert tray came around. Marghie chose the rice pudding, Mrs. Hundert the baked apple. Gabriel got the poached pear. Danny was past eating. "And the bomb sickness afterwards? Not one of you foresaw that. Did you?"

"It is true that this was not anticipated. May I have a glass of buttermilk?" the professor said to the waiter.

"Dad, don't you see? *Don't you see that we must be good to one another?*" The dining room grew silent. Looks passed among the staff. *"And not make believe that we are gods!"* He waved a finger at his father.

"Yes, Daniel, by all means let us be good to one another," Mrs. Hundert said firmly.

The topic was without end, without end at home and at large. When the professor's buttermilk came, he emptied into it the contents of the sugar bowl, then drank this strange dessert down. With a weary motion of the hand in Danny's direction, evidently a solemn signal to desist, he shifted the talk to his great pastime and unassuageable passion, which was opera. *Die Frau ohne Schatten* last night and, still to come, *Otello* at the matinee and *Pelléas et*

Mélisande that evening; these, not the lecture at Columbia, had been the Hunderts' real inducement for visiting New York.

Wasn't there good opera in Chicago? Gabriel asked, for having seen that Marghie and Danny were collusively silent, he was determined to tide over the awkwardness. Looking off to the far end of the dining room, Danny blinked hard, worked his jaw. Gabriel marveled at the readiness of these emotions, all of them so near the surface; Danny left the stoical stuff — composure, steadiness, grace under fire — to his sister.

"Opera in Chicago? Of course, of course," said Hundert, "but not *enough* opera, not as here." He glanced his wife's way, hummed a scrap of what awaited them at Broadway and Sixty-fourth Street, then sang it: *"Esultate! L'orgoglio musulmano sepolto è in mar."* (Evidently, singing in public was a family trait.)

"We saw a catastrophic *Otello* last year at the Lyric," Lilo said to Gabriel, seeking for fairer weather. "During the second act, Desdemona fell deathly ill. On fifteen minutes' notice, someone else stepped in to replace her."

"Poor Desdemona lost a hundred pounds," said the professor, "but it did not save her marriage." He threw up his head in sudden glee, then looked gravely at his wristwatch. "Curtain at two." He urged all of them from the dining room and down the stairs.

Out front, Gabriel shook hands with the Hunderts in a blur of civility and family stress. Hundert pointed his cherry stick at the sky, a debonair way of hailing a cab. Mrs. Hundert tied on a head scarf against the late autumn air, then laid a hand on Hundert's arm. However fleeting, this picture of connubial friendship sank deep. "We'll see you tomorrow morning, my dears!" she called out the window of the cab. Gabriel felt a surge of pleasure go over him, sensing his inclusion in the endearment, for she'd met his gaze as she said it. Here were the due and rightful origins — bluntly, the parents he ought to have had. Here was how marriage ought to be, two on their way, she loving him for dangers he had passed, he loving her that she pitied them. Here was the exchange of modulated views never heard on Terpsichore Street. Here were wonders, he saw them plain, forgetting altogether, this authority on Shakespeare, that, before the curtain falls, Othello and Desdemona must be the death of each other.

————

As if wishing sufficed, they came back to Swarthmore to learn that a fat, lazy guy, Craig Pearlstein, had suddenly gone south, packed his belongings and left, saying the place wasn't for him. Blessings on you, Pearlstein, and thanks. Gabriel now had a room of his own, like the big kids.

Winter took hold, brilliant and clear. One fine evening a call came for him on the hall phone. It was Professor Van Kieft notifying each of his twelve students that there would be something extraordinary to see that night at Sproul Observatory. "Three thirty, shall we say? Be prompt."

Gabriel set his alarm, tried to sleep a little. Not a chance, for he knew what was up — Venus at her greatest westward distance from the sun, very high before dawn. An uncommon smoothness of the air that night would make for optimal viewing.

He'd taken immediately to the sharp northern climate and, walking now to Sproul, filled his lungs happily. The snowfalls were pure pleasure. He loved cutting across the drifts, and loved, after a day of sun and then a drop in temperature, how the crust gave way so pleasantly underfoot. He was in a generalized state of love, and high on his list, along with the weather and the campus and Danny and Marghie, was Sproul. Architecture builds nothing more romantic than observatories, with their visionary instruments and wheeling domes and opening shutters — the galactic catbird's seat. Gabriel had seen photos of the renowned telescopes at Birr

Castle and Mount Wilson and Palomar Mountain and Mount Hopkins and Mauna Kea, each mightier in resolving power than the one before it. One could not revere enough these far-off plots of sacred ground. But Sproul, pokey and obscure, was here and his, the creak of the oaken floor when the instrument was pivoted, the night air pouring in through the aperture, the ring of voices in the dome, along with something less specifiable but intensely present, laid on by the decades, an accumulated benignity you felt there.

Venus showed full face not crescent that night, lustrous silver but with a darker equatorial streak smeared through. And there to behold — all four of them visible — was her diadem of moons. At the eyepiece, Professor Van Kieft was jubilant under combed-over hair. ("I've never seen a comb-over like that," Marghie had noted, "originating from so far down. And he's not yet out of his thirties. And not a bad-looking man. So young and so combed-over. I hear General McArthur, towards the end, had to comb it up from his *armpit*! Van Kieft will too, poor guy.")

Professor Van Kieft dismissed class a little before daybreak. Gabriel walked back down the hill, his feet making light of the snow, and headed for Danny's room.

Grinning aslant and minus the glasses, he glanced either way down the hall, then yanked Gabriel inside, pressed their mouths together, slipped both hands into his jeans. "How's my boy?"

"We saw Venus."

"You saw *Venus*?" Danny adopted for erotic purposes the tones of a patient parent, asking questions, coaxing responses, registering approval. He'd call Gabriel *pal* or *buddy* or *sport* or *tiger,* and in this same good-fatherly register would sometimes tell him to bow down and kiss his feet.

After love Gabriel was chirpy, newsy. Danny tended to drop off. Snores came within a few minutes of the finish. But this morning it was Danny who chirped. "You know what goes on at the Crum after one or two? In good weather, I mean. I've seen as many as three or four guys down there with their pants open."

Gabriel propped himself on one elbow. "Their pants open?"

"Guys you wouldn't expect to see. I don't think I should mention any names. But if you guess right I'll tell you."

Gabriel cuddled up. "Just how many names do you have, Senator McCarthy? How about, say, Tim Bresnahan?"

"Dream on."

"Seth Lippincott?"

"Strictly likes the girls."

"Will Satterthwaite?"

"These aren't realistic guesses. These are your wish list."

"Phinney Debevoise?"

"Phinney has yet to get his first hard-on."

"Chip Duraney?" Silence. "Chip Duraney, I said."

"Chip was there."

"You did him? You can tell me." Silence. "When?" Silence. *"When?"*

"Last year."

"Okay, now we're getting somewhere. Robby Spitznagel?"

"Reliably hetero."

"Paul Rosenzweig?"

"A good bet, but I haven't seen him."

"Randy Schoellkopf?"

"Randy lives down there."

"What *is* it about these Jewish homosexuals? Do you think they're more willing to do that type of thing?"

"They?"

"We."

"Throughout recorded time, Gabe, guys have been finding out-of-the-way spots for 'that type of thing.' Prehistorically, too, I'm sure. The Jews pioneered in ethical monotheism. Isn't that enough for you? We also have to have invented the circle jerk? What's this mania of yours, anyhow, always wanting to know the *Jewish* contribution to everything?"

"I don't do that."

"You *do*."

"Really?"

"You do."

"I'll stop."

"Oh, you're not obnoxious about it. You're not like this shitty little paper in Chicago, *The Hebrew Light*. If a plane goes down and a hundred-fifty people get killed, the headline in *The Light* says, 'Eight Jews Die in Crash!' Makes me sick."

Gabriel tried here to reestablish perfect concord with a kiss, but Danny said, "No kissing unless I say so."

"Why not?"

" 'Cause you're kind of smelly."

"So are you."

They kissed.

"And now, Gabe, I have a very serious question for you."

"Yes?"

"Can you tell me —"

"Yes?"

"— how many Jews got in on the invention of the whoopee cushion? I believe it was a big classified operation. Must have been a lot of Jews involved."

"Shut up."

"Shut up yourself."

They slept away the forenoon, missed classes. Gabriel had to pee, but there were voices in the hall, and Danny didn't want him to be seen emerging with matted hair and sleep in his eyes. Each time he tried to get out of bed, Danny would encircle him with an arm and leg. "You're not going anywhere." On the fourth try, Gabriel got his feet onto the rug — an American flag Danny had spread over the linoleum floor, and this bothered Gabriel.

"It's a desecration to walk on the flag," he said.

"Glad you get the point."

"Maybe it's something Jewish American in me that —"

"Here we go."

"— that senses a violation. When I would stay up late watching TV, and the station would sign off with 'The Star-Spangled Banner' and a picture of the flag, I always got up and stood at attention, even if all I had on was my underwear."

"What this flag's good for is wiping my feet on, you hear? When it's worn out, I'll wipe my butt with it. If you don't mind, that is."

"I wish you wouldn't talk like that."

A knock at the door. "Dan?" It was Marghie. "Open up."

"Go 'way." He looked at Gabriel and put a finger to his lips.

"Have you seen Gabe?"

"No."

"Open up."

"No."

"Why not?"

"Because I don't feel good."

"You know what, I think Gabe's *in* there."

"He's not!"

"Then open up."

"No."

"Why not?"

"BECAUSE!"

"Gabe, listen to me."

"He's not here."

"Gabe, listen. The dean's office has been looking for you all morning."

"Not here, not here. Go 'way," Danny said.

"Gabe, Muriel Binstock said the hall phone rang and rang and woke everybody up. Gabe, listen —"

"HE'S NOT HERE!"

"Gabe, your father's had a heart attack. You mother wants you home."

———

The doctors offered little encouragement. In childhood, Gabriel had prayed early and often for Milton Geismar's death. Even in his atheistic teens, he would inwardly beseech the nonexistent God to strike down that fulminating ignoramus — part Johnson and part Nixon, both of whom seemed crypto-Jewish to Gabriel. The rabbi combined LBJ's sermonic, honeyed-over gloom with Nixon's sweaty vindictiveness. (Oh, for a Kennedyesque father, riding to hounds, sailing before the wind!) From his unpredictable wrath and unappeasable self-pity the rebbitzin had taken refuge in sickness. During the sixteen years of Gabriel's life she'd undergone the following: removal of a recurrent growth from her larynx, hysterectomy, spinal fusion, kidney-stone removal (twice), hemorrhoidectomy, removal of skin cancers and melanomas from her face and arms, removal of polyps from the large bowel. A lot of her had been removed, one way and another. Most recently, there had been a mysterious operation on her tear ducts. Anybody that variously and nonlethally sick, that often, raises at least the suspicion that she is being made so by somebody else. And who, Gabriel demanded to know, had created the toxic environment in which she declined? You! he screamed mentally at the unctuous villain who claimed always to have his wife's interests at heart but was in fact her mortal enemy; who had, by the atmosphere he created, kept her in such a bad way.

His father could in any dispute say to him, *"Look* what you're *doing* to your *mother!"* As this man, who privately rubbed his hands together when financial ruin overtook a wealthy congregant or lit up like a firefly when sexual foibles pulled people down to disgrace, had found in schadenfreude his heart's ease, so his wife found hers in illnesses. And as he honored her battery of strange ailments, so she revered his infected estimation of people. Thus the covenant uniting them.

After six days in intensive care, the doctors sent the rabbi home with a practical nurse. No candidate for bypass, they said. He asked for kasha bow ties with milk. The rebbitzin brought him a bowl of the bow ties and a glass of milk. "Together!" he howled, and started to cry, and sent the bow ties flying.

"I'll give you something to cry about," Gabriel heard himself say. It was the very line his father had, ten and twelve years ago, threatened him with. Here the son of a bitch was, helpless in bed with an oxygen feed to his nose. Go ahead. Gabriel got the belt, the very one, from the rabbi's closet and laid into him with blows. The nurse leapt in and wrested the belt from Gabriel, not without getting ladders in her hose and wrecking her starched hat, for he gave her a tussle. She didn't want to work in a house like that, she said. She'd inform the agency to send someone else.

The new nurse arrived, speaking a spicy Cajun, chatting in low tones on the telephone, watching her afternoon shows while her patient watched the wall. She discussed with him, one-sidedly, Christmas preparations. Having been forewarned by the agency that a mad youth was in the house, she gave Gabriel a wide berth. During one brief spell when she was off the phone, it had a chance to ring. Gabriel snatched up the receiver. Marghie, calling from the heart of a Chicago blizzard. "We may get disconnected," she said.

"Is Dan there?" asked Gabriel.

"Never heard of him."

"Come on, Marg."

"Ask about me first. Say 'How are you, Marghie?' Say 'I hope you're having a nice holiday.' Say 'Marg, is every little thing all right?' "

"Is every little thing —"

"No."

"What's wrong?"

"Now's the first time Danny and I are in love with the same person."

"Dan's in love with me?"

"You rat."

"Marg —"

"You rat."

"I love you every way but one, Marg. It's not you. It's the female anatomy. It's as remote from me as Timbuktu."

"Oh, Gabe, someday you might actually *visit* Timbuktu!" She hung up.

He called her back. "Let me talk to Dan, please."

"Not home."

"Tell him to call me when he gets in."

"*If* he gets in."

"Meaning?"

"Meaning he's lit out."

"For where?"

"Never says. Scrapes together a little money, sometimes honestly, sometimes not, and goes. We've received phone calls from Tierra del Fuego, Ulan Bator, et cetera. You think I'm joking?"

Silence.

"He did run away once to New Harmony, and another time to Muskegon."

"May I speak with him please?"

"He's in São Paulo."

"Marg —"

"He's in Nome." She hung up.

He called her back. At the other end, no hello, no nothing. "Please," he said. Compact silence. "Please, Marg."

"HE'S NOT HERE!" It was the truth. Danny hadn't been heard from for days. It was not the first time. Even as a little boy he'd give them the slip at the Museum of Science and Industry or at the Art Institute. Once at the model yacht basin he wandered off. Lilo and Marghie called frantically for him. No Danny. Several hours later they did find him, surrounded by concerned adults in Burnham Park and happily pretending to speak only Hungarian. "We don't know where he is. We're worried."

He could tell now she wasn't lying. "I'm worried too."

"The line's breaking up, can you hear? It's this blizzard we're having."

"Sounds okay at this end."

"We may get cut off. It's just terrible, all this static."

"I don't hear a thing, Marg."

The receiver buzzed in his hand.

———

Twelve days later, at the turn of the year, Milton Geismar complained while receiving a sponge bath that in his hands was a needling sensation and that everybody's voice sounded tinny and far-off. "I'm scared," he told the new nurse, "of my only child, who beats me." She dried him, then applied an anti-inflammatory to a couple of bedsores on his flank. Craning around to see, the rabbi let out a sob. She covered him, reinserted his IV. The rebbitzin, who volunteered her Wednesdays at the temple gift shop, was not home yet. The nurse went down the hall and asked Gabriel to come and sit with his father while she went on her break. He said he would, he would, but just this minute was reading in *The Insect World of J. Henri Fabre* about how the glowworm, its lantern-tail pulsing with pleasure, uses a hidden mandible to crack open snails and feed on them. (This was slumming, to be sure; entomology was kids' stuff. It stirred in him abysmal memories of the torment he'd inflicted on bugs when little. Fabre was his penance and idle pleasure.) He was reading about how the long-horned beetle grub tunnels into the heartwood of an oak. About the snail-shell bee, the bembex wasp, the foamy cicadella, the thistle weevil, and about how newly hatched Narbonne Lycosa spiders, by means of an instinct that shows itself but once and then vanishes, climb and climb to the highest point they can reach . . . The nurse flounced out for a smoke.

Somewhere in the house there sounded a little signal — distant, it seemed, but he could hear it. It was like a baby puling. No, whining. Or more like wailing. No, more like a lambish bleat. Gabriel put down his Fabre. What was it? Was it *bleat, bleat* he'd heard, or was it more like, for instance, "help, help" — emitted hollowly, as if on the intake of breath? Gabriel bolted from his chair. Coming into the hall, as in a dream where there's power neither to flee nor scream, Gabriel saw the oxygen feed raised in one hand as his father flailed, drowning in the air.

The rabbi went slack on his feet, but did not fall. Gabriel wondered, *Was it true people sometimes die standing up, stand dead awhile before keeling over. Was he dead, then?*

Like an ironing board Milton Geismar fell forward, as if in answer. He didn't declare, before going down, any patriarchal imprecation such as, "I cut you off forever!" or "I'm not so easy to kill!" or "Bastard!" or "Wander in darkness, no son of mine!" He served no everlasting bill of attainder. Gabriel saw on the carpet a stain spread from his father's mouth and nose, claret colored, nearly black. He fulfilled now his duty, or tried to, but could not remember whether CPR, in which he'd never been instructed very well, called for fifteen compressions of the chest for every two exhalations into the victim's mouth, or vice versa. Gabriel did both, turning him supine and cocking the head back and putting his mouth to his father's. First, fifteen compressions to two breaths, then, two compressions to fifteen breaths, then — guessing wildly — five breaths to five compressions, none of it availing. He did not stop, would not till that cursed nurse came back. What occurred to him as he labored, strange to say, was the old method he'd read about of dealing with a parricide — the malefactor placed in a sack with a dog and a viper and thrown into the sea. He pleaded: *Let her not walk in on this, not Mother, please don't make her see this . . .*

What does fate spare you? Nothing today. He heard footsteps he knew on the stairs and lifted his bloodied mouth. "Mom, we need an ambulance!"

———

The funeral was less than twenty-four hours later, very early in the day, very simple — without eulogy, at Gabriel's insistence; he got no argument from his mother. In the wilder moments of inward rage, he'd dreamed of rising to memorialize his father, telling the congregation that Milton Geismar was a domestic ghoul. Or of arranging the disgrace of a cremation and bringing the urn of ashes to temple and spilling them deliberately. In the event, it was all he could do to thank the long line of condolers who shook his hand and said what a blessing Rabbi Geismar had been in their lives. Lillian Rose and Irving Raimey, whose son had died several years back of Hodgkin's disease, broke down completely, telling how without Milton Geismar they couldn't have borne their loss.

"Our Stevie, *olev ha shalom*," Irving said, and could say no more.

"When our Stevie passed away," said Lillian Rose, "we decided not to go to the funeral. I mean, we were crazy. We were sick in our minds with anger and I'll tell you something, young man, I hated every woman whose precious baby wasn't dead. Crazy with a mother's grief. And Irving was crazy too and we hated everybody and most of all we hated each other."

"It's enough, Rose," her husband said, wiping his eyes.

"I've started, Irv, and I'll finish. It was your father, Gabe, who said to us if we didn't go to our baby's funeral we'd end up hating ourselves too much. And he was right, he was right! Oh God, Irving, get me something, I feel so bad. Get me a Pepsi."

Another mother and father, Jane and Melvin Kleimist, had a son who'd been seized by marauders on his way to Machu Picchu, and mailed home a finger at a time. And another couple, Pearl and Maurice Kaufman, had lost their daughter in a mountain climbing incident. It happened in a remote part of Idaho, and she had to be helicoptered out. Milton Geismar stayed up all night with the stricken parents and drove them to the airport the following afternoon to receive their daughter's body. Gabriel remembered his father at dinner shaking his head, saying Jewish children were nowadays getting as careless of their lives as the most brainless goyim. "How lucky you were, young fellow, to have had a *great* man for a father!" Pearl Kaufman said.

"He was quite a guy," said Maurice, crushing Gabriel to him.

"Quite a guy, yes," Gabriel echoed, fighting for air in Maury's grip.

His mother rested her weight on him only once, when they got back home. She'd said very little since Geismar died. She'd wept comfortably, more or less steadily. Now she leaned on him with what sounded like a terminal exhalation. "Mom, brace up."

She composed herself, went to the living room. "You need some help, Mom?" She took a framed pen-and-ink portrait of her late husband from the wall. She opened the back of the frame, took out the drawing. "Mom, what are you doing?" She shook it out and went into the kitchen. He heard her rummage around, then heard

the back door open and shut. He moved to the window. "Mom!"
But she'd already set fire to the picture.

"*Mom, what are you doing?*" he hollered through the glass.

"*I never liked this ugly thing!*" she hollered back.

two

LIGHTNING IN A BOTTLE

Turned out the old guy had salted away a fortune. The rebbitzin's health bloomed, perking up as soon as probate of the rabbi's will disclosed the handsome profit a small investment in Communications Satellite Corporation, on its initial public offering, had reaped over the years. Rowena Geismar got a hairdo and wardrobe to suit her changed status and frame of mind. She spoke of "the new me" and didn't care what people thought; played rummy and canasta, developing a formidable gift for the latter particularly; went with women friends on kosher cruises; consented, indeed, after fifteen minutes of reflection, to a glamorous nonkosher cruise when some highly Reform and very rich widows invited her along — two weeks in the Cyclades and Dodecanese. Rowena rode a burro up the Santorini switchbacks; on Crete, saw the palace at Knossos and entered the Idaian cave where Zeus was reared; on Mykonos, bought a loose-knit sweater; saw the stone lions at Delos; on Naxos saw the giant *kouros*; on Rhodes saw little boys snatching newborn crayfish out of the harbor shallows and popping them into their mouths; ate some strange things herself. She phoned from Patmos to see how Gabriel was.

Fine, more than fine, and packing for Wisconsin. His summer internship at Sproul did not begin till mid-July. "You'll come to us meantime, won't you?" Mrs. Hundert had said in a letter. "There's the lake for swimming and all of Wisconsin for hiking and many of our favorite people. Should you get bored you could go away. It's not just Margaret and Daniel, it's Grisha and myself. We want you among us, dear Gabriel." For this he had intrigued, and it had come to pass. "You are *required*, let us say, and say no more about it. With love." Those wishing to grant anchorage know well enough how to fetch those in need of it. He began to grasp that Hundert life was hers to superintend, as presently his own would be. No withstanding Lilo. Besides, he wanted desperately to go, despite a terse warning from Marghie: "Nothing possibly in the least ever happens here." (He remembered how she'd moon around Swarthmore saying that, without attribution till some other cinéaste had called her on the line, which was from *Philadelphia Story*.)

Gabriel's mathematical diary, all calculation up to now, burst into words:

7 v 71: En route. One night last spring, Marg pulled the Bible off her shelf. I didn't know what for a minute. Thought she'd turned holy. It was just a game of hers. You open up at random, put your finger on a line, and figure out its pertinence. Marg knows this is about as useful as reading tea leaves but loves it just the same, even though she's not very good at it. Always gets the begats or some other boring thing, or some New Testamentary treacle. I tried only once. Let the book fall open, brought my finger down, and "God setteth the solitary in families" was what it said.

Later. Certainly not saving any dough by taking the train. Dislike of planes, however. Root of problem may be account I read of how people behave when a plane's going down. How a man will (pointlessly) grab hold of a woman or child to buffer the impact. Would not want to behave like that, and think I would.

Enough money (just) to have a couchette instead of sitting up all night. Plenty of zweiback in a plastic bag, plenty of seltzer water. Pleasant sensation of being sealed up. Who are they who sleep in their coffins in order to practice being dead? Turn off the lights, raise the shade, watch the nation speed past. Coffin with a view. Lots of coffin-dwellers all through the centuries, I believe. Look it up.

Same night, 3:00: Can't sleep. Remembering about Mom, how when she heard of a death in the community, however she felt, however sick, would go to the kitchen and bake a cheesecake. Daddy had only to come home with a certain set to his jaw and flash at her his despising eyes (despising of death, I mean) and say, "Cheesecake, honey," and she'd head for the kitchen. Sometimes fruit-covered, blueberries or strawberrries, sometimes plain. I remember how I loved her turquoise Mixmaster and hanging around while she mixed.

Daybreak: Indiana whizzing by. Excellent dream just now. At our house Dick and Pat, Lyndon and Lady Bird, Jack and Jackie — the colossi and their consorts. All worse for wear. Dad's day-nurse, the second one, is there too. So Lyndon gets hold of me and takes me aside and says, very hangdog, "Have you noticed, Gabe, what a distant second Father's Day is to Mother's?" "As it SHOULD be, Mr. President!" I reply, and he releases me.

Gabriel knew he was headed for a Nobel. A shoo-in. Where were his friends going? Danny was a substitute lifeguard at the lake, Marghie put in listless time at a gift shop in Portage. These were unenterprising jobs, and the lack of enterprise was a source of tension between father and son, as between mother and daughter. The professor lectured Danny, but gave Marghie the benefit of the doubt. Mrs. Hundert did the reverse. "Not what you went to college for," he said to him and she to her. But what had occurred to Gabriel was that Danny and Marghie might be permanent children, a pair of sprites exempt from development, and that their Peter Pannery might be something Lilo and Grisha quietly rejoiced in, despite the lectures.

A bus from Chicago deposited him at three that afternoon. There was Danny shirtless at the station. No underwear either, as was plain to see through a pair of nylon shorts. "We fought about who was coming to get you. I won." A big bear hug but no kiss. This was the sticks.

"You put the kibosh on underwear or something?" The pikestaff in Danny's shorts grew plainer, as if in answer. What also could not be ignored was the reek of him. "And you're *fierce*." Gabriel approved of this pungent microclimate that went everywhere with Dan. "Fierce from your armpits."

"I'll shower."

"Not too often, please."

"Everybody complains. Mom, Marghie."

"Let 'em."

Danny took Gabriel's backpack and duffel bag and put them in the rear seat of the Hundert car, a legendary vehicle, a fifty-nine Studebaker sedan. "Runs on rubber bands and a prayer. You could say Mom and Dad put their money on the wrong horse. Getting spare parts for this thing's no joke. Should've gone for a Packard, or a Nash Rambler."

They passed into the cow-dotted countryside, the Studebaker hesitating ominously between first and second gear, grinding between second and third, then jackrabbiting.

"You sure you know how to drive a standard?"

"It's all I've ever driven, Gabe. I take that as a slur."

"Look, *automatic* is all *I've* ever driven."

"Minty boy."

"Pardon?"

"Minty. Faggy. You sound like a fag when you say things like that."

"Nowadays we say 'gay,' Dan."

"Have it my way. 'Fag' suits us both." The transmission agonized under them. "Let's just come out of the closet this weekend, what do you say? Shake up the joint. Might be a relief. But then what? You're edited down, a caricature. That's what coming out of the closet means. Getting turned into one thing only."

"Well, I think the closet may be busting up around us."

The car moaned and leapt. Through the side mirror, Gabriel saw a dirty plume of exhaust spread out behind them.

"Just pray to this heap. We're nearly home." They passed down a dirt road leading to an appealing pair of houses — Arts and Crafts, roughly speaking — built of redwood and stone and graced with living porches, sturdy, comfortable, no-nonsense dwellings, separated by an open meadow along the lakeshore. "Here's our place," Danny said of the lesser structure. "Over there's where the Dunallens live. Our landlords, here for the whole summer. You may like them better than I do. Wait'll you meet the odd wad who's staying with them." Out of the lesser house bounded Lilo and Grisha, full of greetings and queries. Marghie, from a dormer, added her subdued hello.

"Something," Danny said, "has got her in a snit. It's not you. It's something she read about the studios not transferring nitrate negatives to safety stock. This morning at breakfast she recited the names of several hundred lost masterpieces of American cinema. I told her to *can* it, and that made Dad laugh, at least."

Grisha embraced Gabriel heartily, mopped his brow. "A cool day by the Louisiana standard. But we Wisconsinians call this hot." The Hunderts, evidently, had been in seasonal residence long enough to regard Portage and environs as a part of native ground. The house was rented to them by Elise and Edward Dunallen. Ned hailed originally from Terre Haute, and had passed the summers of his youth here at the lakeshore. In New York, he was fiction editor at a famously high-nosed magazine. (As usual, Gabriel had been to the library to do a little research.) Ned had edited, in his day,

William Measler, bard of Anglo-Saxon woes among the club-car classes of the Atlantic northeast; D.B. Cronebacher, wrathful, not-to-be-photographed recluse who, having delighted millions with four books, was nowadays as silent as the tomb; Lorena Fraley, greathearted Mississippi spinster, a Vesuvius at home; rapier-tongued Nellie McNaughton, much feared dark lady of American letters; Eamon O'Gorman, professionally Irish ear-bender, whose real name was something else; Millicent Selby Whitcomb, English lesbian Communist who lived in Dorset and wrote endlessly about elves; Dimitri Galinov, incomparably gifted Russian émigré who, in the wake of titanic financial success, lived out old age in a Swiss hotel; Ralph Turnspike, prolific in all genres, white hope of his generation, who dwelled north of Boston and was regarded *inter alia* as the high-nosed magazine's, and therefore the nation's, most redoubtable book reviewer. These and many more of renown were edited by Dunallen. Though their books were a mystery to Gabriel, their names were familiar. Even devoted non-readers of fiction knew of Cronebacher and Turnspike. Galinov had written a work of high art so scandalous in its premise that the whole world got wind of it. Miss Fraley, heralded Mother Goose of us all, was as welcome on the talk shows as any rock star.

Only the truly deprived were ignorant of these names. But Dunallen was another matter. Ned had made no more splash than a rose petal dropped down a well. And yet by the lights of the discerning few he, also, was a great writer. As Marghie had recently explained it to Gabriel, there were writers, and writer's writers, and writer's writer's writers, and Dunallen was in this third and presumably final category of rarity. (If there was a writer's writer's writer's writer he hadn't come to light yet and was in any case too rarified to bear thinking about.) A devoted handful regarded Edward Dunallen as the hidden king of American writing, a mighty artist not granted his due, a secret. His books were all but secret, anyhow. The world knew Dunallen, despite many publications, as merely an editor, merely the crossroads where Galinov, Turnspike, Cronebacher, and the rest intersected.

"According to Mom and Dad," Marghie had said, "Ned's a genius mistaken for a Sunday scribbler. Mom says 'if people would only open those books and read them' and on and on. So I did. I went to the library and there they were. One of them somebody had actually checked out, in 1958. On the strength of that I borrowed it myself. And liked it a lot. Lemme tell you what that book's about."

He begged her not to.

"Oh Gabe, I feel a plot summary coming on."

He begged her. Three months later, what should Gabriel have in his duffel bag but that very copy of Dunallen's *As the Twig Is Bent*, badly overdue. Something about her synopsis had got to him, and he'd gone to the library for a look. (From the point of view of the book, patient on its shelf, this must have been stupendous. Two readers in as many years after the long disuse.) He wondered how so much had been smuggled past the customs in 1945. Here was a story of first love and first loss, and the lovers were boys. Sure, it purported to tell only of friendship, two youths edging each other toward the rituals of courtship and matrimony. A couple of flimsy girl characters turn up. But euphemism and ellipsis could not veil Dunallen's forbidden subject matter. Even as resolute a nonreader of novels as Gabriel got the picture. Friendship? "Compy Fredericks" *cuts his throat* for love of "Skip Aldrich." Since when do friends do that?

"Gabriel, let's get you settled," Lilo said. "Your room is the corner one, up the stairs and down the hallway."

The house and its contents belonged to the Dunallens and, despite fifteen years of summer residence by the Hunderts, had retained the strong Presbyterian stamp of the former: hooked rugs, straight-backed cane-bottomed chairs, sofas in faded chintz, iron bedsteads, crocheted bureau scarves, here and there a flourish of philodendron. In the living room, Parcheesi, Monopoly, Clue, Sorry!, and Candyland were stacked under a side table. Above the mantel hung an engraving of a ruined abbey in Solway Firth, as the legend underneath declared. No, this was not the Hunderts' house.

And yet, with nothing in their bearing to suggest that it was their own property they were stepping onto, to dinner that evening came the Dunallens. Ned and Elise had been the Hunderts' landlords pure and simple fifteen years ago, but for a long time now had been their closest friends. "A very superior slice of American life," was how Grisha described them. Superior in cultivation, in judgment, in manners — manners, indeed, from another time. The Dunallen daughters, Deirdre and Fiona, when small had been accustomed to greet their elders with a curtsy. (Marghie, older and skeptical of such airs and graces, mocked them one evening with a slow malicious curtsy and frozen smile of her own, and had been scolded. "Silly geese!" she'd hollered over the banister as Lilo hustled her up the stairs. Never had Danny loved his sister more than on that night.) Grisha and Lilo marveled at having such exemplars to hand. As for the view from the other end of the meadow, it was evidently as admiring. There had not, in all these summers, been any difficulty or misunderstanding. The Hunderts and the Dunallens were exceptionally careful of each other. Between them a reciprocal guardianship had grown up. Indeed, each marriage had come to rely on the other. "I married the most extraordinary, most unaccountable man I've ever met," said Elise Dunallen to Lilo Hundert. "And I think you did too." While Ned Dunallen to Grisha Hundert: "Can there be two nobler women, Grisha, than our young wives, two comelier or more all-knowing?" Each couple was for the other a stay against ordinariness, each a glorifying mirror and recollection of original hope. While the Hunderts' gaze was on the Dunallens, and vice versa, an ideal flourished.

Elise emerged now from the meadow, swinging a bottle of wine in either hand. The afternoon had waned to a clear gold light. Girlishly beautiful, she seemed more daughter than wife to the raw-boned sunken-faced fellow beside her. He put up his hand for a visor, appeared to say something. Smoothing down her skirt with the bottles, Elise nodded and flashed a sudden smile. Marghie's capsule sketch had included that Elise was a timber heiress from Seattle. "A Knowles. They clear-cut whole stretches of the Pacific Northwest," she said. "Their own land and, if you looked the other way, yours too. Anyhow, she came straight down from Wellesley to the various New York editorial offices, looking for a position. And Ned was one of the people who interviewed her. This is what is known in Hollywood as Meeting Cute. Before long old Ned was sizing Ellie up for a different sort of job. He popped the question on their third date."

Here Marghie changed her tone. "Turned out she was on the rebound." Straight dope as follows: Elise Knowles had come to town and, looking as she did, made a sensation. The nation's best-known movie critic, John Burgee, a married man and drunkard and law unto himself, and author of *A World to Win*, his account of Depression-era tenant farmers in Alabama, came calling. Elise didn't stand a chance.

In the wake of Burgee, Dunallen must have looked a reprieve. Whatever else, Ned was no womanizer. He courted in the old high way of love. How else, seeing as what he knew of the practice came wholesale out of books? Ned Dunallen, who had only loved men, was in need of a wife. Psychoanalysis had prepared him for the tests of courtship, the rigors of matrimony. Away he went with the training wheels still on, and careered into a heartsick timber heiress from Seattle, who'd certainly deserved better from her New York adventure than once around the track with that cad Burgee. (Lilo had gradually told Marghie all of this, or enough that she inferred the rest. "Do the Dunallens know as much about you and Dad?" No answer, only her mother's could-mean-anything smile, as Marghie peered for an instant into depths unknown.)

Bringing up the rear was their houseguest, and a bit of a parson by the disapproving look he seemed to cast on Hundertdom. Gabriel came down the front steps for introductions. "None of your 'Mister' and 'Missus,' young fellow. Here at the lake we're Ellie and Ned," said the old guy, eyes alight. But he was frail, with bones that ground together in his hand when Gabriel shook it. His skin looked like pink tissue paper. His benevolent smile showed carious teeth. Could this wreck survive till Labor Day? And yet he was boyish — in his curiosity, his readiness to know someone new. "Meet our friend Peter Storrow," said Ned. Peter Storrow extended a dead fish and put on a schoolmasterish frown. He looked mildly surprised to find himself among people of uncertain credentials. He was making the best of it by being polite, imagining formulaic courtesy and politeness to be the same thing. Gabriel reeled quietly with the realization that someone he was ready to like simply didn't like him. Or anybody else in the lesser house, it seemed. Condescending to visit this riff-raff next door, mere summer tenants, not the real right thing, not Dunallens, he discharged a duty, but only had eyes for Elise and Ned. As you wish, Gabriel said to himself and grinned back. A word he'd never had the slightest use for till now suggested itself: courtier — here was a courtier. Gabriel had not met one before unless, he mused, he was maybe a courtier himself.

Dry martinis loosened the tongues of the grown-ups. The tongues of the young ran free on beer. Lilo warmed a cream of sorrel soup, and rubbed a butterflied leg of lamb with garlic and sage before Grisha grilled it. Bottles of red wine, kindness of Elise and Ned, were opened to breathe. Over the course of a decade Lilo Hundert had prepared every single recipe in volume one of

Child, Bertholle, and Beck's *Mastering the Art of French Cooking.*
How many other wives could put hand to heart and make such a
claim? She took food seriously, said if the food was good the rest of
life stood a better chance of being good too. There was a gratin of
potatoes, onions, and anchovies. Salad from the garden followed.
Dessert was banana cream pie.

Marghie had Elise's ear all through dinner. She was inveighing
against Louis B. Mayer. She said Orson Welles's woes were owing
to him. Said Mayer had truckled to the Hearst conglomerate and
to Hearst's filthy dirty mouthpiece, Louella Parsons. Elise bowed
her head in awe of this invective. How ardently the young did care
about what they cared about. Marghie said Mayer, acting on behalf
of all the major studio heads, tried to get the negative and prints
of *Citizen Kane* destroyed, so fearful were they of Hearst and of
what Louella, acting on Hearst's orders, might write about certain
of their leading stars. Besides, Louis B. very much liked his place at
the San Simeon table.

Gabriel liked his place at the table here in Wisconsin. He was
seated next to Ned, whose decrepitude you tended to forget, despite
what he was saying: "When you reach my stage of life, the older
generation are completely gone. What's happened year by year is
you've turned into them, even if inwardly you don't feel it. And I
don't. Everybody's got an inner age which does not change. Mine is
seventeen. Seventeen till I die."

"Mine is seventy-one!" Grisha called from his end of the table.
"I am superb in the role of old man, having rehearsed the part all
my life!"

Lilo was back and forth between the kitchen and the dining
room.

"Mom, can I help?" Danny asked.

"Such a *good* boy," Marghie said.

"You may take the potatoes out of the oven, Daniel, and you may carve the lamb. Then you may cut a little chive for garnish," Lilo said, and made a tight face at Marghie.

Grisha had Peter the Silent on his left, and was trying mightily to draw him out. He was accustomed to young people who knew who he was and took an interest in him. This young literatus seemed never to have heard of physics itself, much less of Gregor Hundert. Not a hanging offense, but he didn't seem to have heard of much else either. Was Ned really going to make a writer of him? What exactly would he write *about*? "Tell me, young man, have you been to the Southwest? Lilo and I spent several years in New Mexico, as you may know." Peter didn't know, or care, evidently. "Our travel in those times was rather restricted, on account of the work I was doing, but when we could get away we would wisit the Anasazi ruins. They are throughout the Four Corners."

"Four Corners?" Peter asked.

He was really too much, this fool. "Where the right angles of New Mexico, Arizona, Utah, and Colorado meet, my boy. You might write something about these eleventh- and twelfth-century Americans. The current ethnographical materials are full of doubtful claims. Someone like yourself, without an ax to grind and coming fresh to the experience, could do something worthwhile. Ned, Ned, this boy should write about the Anasazi!"

"What a good idea," Ned averred, and at this Peter brightened. Ned's imprimatur was evidently all he needed. "Ellie and I went to Mesa Verde with the girls some years back. I dream about it to this day."

"Oh, yes," said Grisha. "Everyone who's been there dreams about it. Did you go to Balcony House? That's the one I seem to dream about. There is a wery narrow corridor you must pass through. People grow panicky in there. I did, I am bound to say, and as Lilo can testify. Such is my dream. I am immobilized in that tiny space with my girth, my present-day girth, pressing against both walls."

"He was slender as a *wand* when we went there!" Lilo cried from her end of the table.

"Not as you see me now."

Looking back and forth between them, it was borne in on Gabriel how much Peter looked like Ned. For a wild moment he fantasized that this was a bastard son. But from what he knew of Ned Dunallen, it did seem unlikely that he'd left natural issue in his wake. ("That's a lap a *girl* can sit on," said Marghie, "without fear or favor. I'd suggest you boys stay off.") No, it was simply that this Peter Storrow wanted so badly to *be* Ned Dunallen that he'd come to resemble him.

Lilo said: "We went first to Bandelier. Then to Canyon de Chelly. Unforgettable trip."

"We were skinny," Grisha said.

"We were *young*. We didn't care about comfort. Sometimes we slept in the car."

"The Studebaker?" Gabriel asked.

"The Studebaker's great-grandfather," Lilo said.

"I don't mind telling you that I took one look at those cliff dwellings and burst into tears," Ned said.

"Oh, you, of course," said Grisha, eliciting easy laughter all around. Ned was famous for tears. Ned broke down at supermarket grand openings. Tell Ned Dunallen your boy's Little League game had been rained out or ants had got into the picnic hamper and he'd well up. "Waterworks" the locals called him in Portage, not unkindly, for these were the real *lacrimae rerum,* not self-flattery. The Little League, the picnic — such passing mischances found a home in Ned's undimmed heart.

Lilo said, "In Arizona, north of the Black Mesa, is an even more beautiful cliff dwelling, Keet Seel, but strictly for the connoisseur. You come to it after an eight-hour hike down sandy, manure-covered switchbacks. That's the easy part."

"It is the return that is memorable," Grisha said. "We had foolishly drunk most of our water on the way down. Call this the improvidence of youth."

"We were *delirious* with thirst. But it was worth it —"

"Oh, inwigorating!"

"— on account of what we'd seen. The town is nestled deep in an eyelet. The rimrock is massive. The drop to the riverbed is straight down. Only hearty souls make the trip. Once there, you'd swear the inhabitants have left but are coming back. The seven or eight hundred years seem like an afternoon."

Ned asked, "Where did they go? Why? Our tour guide gave a very murky account."

"They went south, roughly speaking. But everybody. Why is conjectural. The tree rings indicate thirty years of drought. But they'd survived that and worse before. There is no evidence whatever of disease. Nor of war. Total migrations are rare, after all. A whole people picking up and leaving like that."

"Perhaps something theological drove them," Ned said. "Some religious compulsion."

Grisha said: "Yes, this is what I think."

Marghie considered the Anasazi a great big bore. In the silver of the pictures, and strictly there, she made her happy home; she'd gone on at her end of the table from Welles to Sturges, specifically *The Lady Eve*. "Barbara Stanwyck and Charles Coburn are cardsharps on a luxury liner, a couple of cuties. Also on board is Henry Fonda, who's a very rich, romantically inexperienced bookworm, their intended victim. He's handsome, he's callow, he's something like you, Peter." But her style of fun was not in his line. Peter looked as if he'd smelled something bad.

By now the grown-up conversation had dwindled down; the floor it seemed was hers. "Scene changes. We are in Connecticut — or Con*neck*ticut, as everybody in this movie says. Have you

noticed how often it's Con*neck*ticut that is the pastoral retreat in
these thirties and forties movies? Anyhow, Stanwyck turns up in
Con*neck*ticut posing as another woman, English and aristocratic,
and Henry Fonda falls for it! A barefaced lie, same dame, as anybody
can see, but Henry buys some malarkey about her and the look-
alike back on the boat being someway sisters, one English, one
American. Puh-leeze! Pointy headed but *dumb* is what the guy is.
Also cute. And you're cheering for him and Barbara, I mean you're
standing in your seat and whooping, when in the last scene he takes
her in his arms and she says, 'Don't you know you're the only man
I've ever loved? Don't you know I couldn't look at another man
if I wanted? Don't you *know* I've been waiting all my life for you,
you big mug?' " It was among Marghie's gifts to become a whole
variety of leading ladies. You saw, by turns, Rosalind Russell, Joan
Crawford, Jean Arthur, Claudette Colbert, Bette Davis flare up in
her. She was fireworks when she got going, and she had got going
now. "Barbara's all done with being a crook and an imposter, and
Henry's all done with being a sap, and they're going to be just fine.
The end."

A smattering of applause from Gabriel and Danny. "Double
feature! Double feature!" cried the latter.

"Requests?" Marghie asked. The conversation of the grown-ups
had been vanquished. They sat with parted lips.

"Lady from Shanghai," said Gabriel.

The impish gleam of Welles was immediately on Marghie. She
asked, with an Irish brogue and sea-doggish sneer, " 'What was I,
Michael O'Hara, doing on a luxury yacht pleasure cruisin' in the
sunny Kerribbean Sea? Why, it's clear now I was chasin' a married
woman. But that's not the way I wanted to look at it. Nooooo. To
be a real prize fathead like Michael O'Hara you've got to swallow
whole all the lies you can tink up to tell yerself.' He's working for a
rattlesnake trial lawyer named Bannister who goes around on two

canes, like this —" She rose to demonstrate. "Guy's married to Rita Hayworth, no less. What's she want with a ramshackle husband like that? Begins with *m*, ends with *y*. Rita's high blonde in this picture. Her hairdo is in the Lana Turner style. All similarity ends there, I hasten to add. Rita is never coy or simpering. Rita makes Lana look like what she is, a bimbo. Anyhow, the whole cast of characters is cooped up on this schooner out of New York, the *Circe*, traveling to San Francisco by way of the canal. This is no ship of fools he's on. He's the only fool. Everybody else on board is scheming to put him in a frame. First words out of Rita's mouth to Orson are 'I don't smoke,' which is a lie, like everything else she says. She tells him to call her Rosalie. Others are inclined to call her Elsa. Her real name may be Circe. She certainly seems to have turned the men around her into something other than men. Orson says, 'Once, off the hump of Brazil, I saw the ocean so darkened with blood it was black and the sun fadin' away over the lip of the sky. All about, the sea was made of sharks and more sharks still.' " Marghie had the accent cold. " 'And no water at all. Ah, the beasts had took to eatin' each other. In their frenzy they ate at themselves. You could smell the death reekin' up out of the sea.' Our sailor boy is brave and gallant but he's a fool, a venturesome fool, a deliberate *intentional* fool. And Rita's playing him, she's the coldest-blooded shark off the hump of Brazil. She's turned him into an A-number-one chump, which is incidentally what she did to Orson in real life. They're on the rocks by the time they make this one. They've got love scores to settle and are doing it in public. Odds are long on O'Hara throughout, but when the picture ends, after many absurd complications, he's the only one without hot lead in him. Rosalie's on the floor, bleeding her life away. 'Everybody is somebody's fool,'" Marghie said now in the brogue. " 'The only way to stay out of trouble is to grow old, so I guess I'll concentrate on that.' And he strides off into the afternoon. Roll credits."

You trembled for her when she launched into one of these stem-winders. She was the lady on the high wire. She was Lillian Gish on the ice floes. She was a soul in peril. If somebody cracks up around here, Gabriel told himself, it's going to be her.

"Way to go Sis," said Danny.

Lilo looked as if she wished her daughter would choose a profession other than plot summary. Grisha said very precisely, "Way to go," relishing the phrase.

She'd let them off easy, Elise felt, who vividly remembered sitting the previous summer through parts one and two of Eisenstein's *Ivan the Terrible*. She put a hand through Marghie's hair. Marghie put her head briefly on Elise's shoulder, looking spent but triumphant.

Peter Storrow's eyes had grown very bright. Of all the goddamned nonsense, thought Gabriel — he's falling in love with Marg.

"If we want to play miniature golf we'd better get going," Danny said, still chewing, rising from the table.

"There's *dessert* to come, Daniel," said Lilo.

"*Marvelous* dessert," Grisha said. "Mother has made it specially."

"Look, Mom, we have to tee off by ten. Can't we just eat dessert when we get back?" In his heart, he was already at the course, putt-putting over a drawbridge that opened and closed at regular intervals, down a narrow strip of green hedged by water hazards, up a chute into a well containing several holes through which your ball dropped to good or ill fortune.

"Coming?" Marghie asked Peter. Or is miniature golf not high-minded enough for you, her scoffing gaze seemed to add. She was formidable, and formidable was not what he was used to in a girl. He was used to namby-pamby types cut from the same bolt of cloth as himself. "It's the best fun up here."

"Okay," said Peter. Oh hell, thought Gabriel. Danny set his jaw.

The young heading out to play miniature golf — was this not sufficient occasion for tears? The door banged shut, the Studebaker disappeared down the drive, and Ned erupted. "For my health," he said, and put out a forfending hand. "It's a heart attack or tears. I pick tears." Lilo knew what the trouble was. She no longer dared ask Elise and Ned how their daughters were. The stricken looks had become too much to bear. Deirdre was at a Sufi compound in upstate New York. Fiona was in a daisy chain in southern California. Their parents hadn't talked to either in more than eight months. Here was cause enough for weeping.

"Your boy and girl are two *miracles*," Ned said to Grisha, wiping his face with the back of his hand. Tight-lipped, dry-eyed, Elise stared into her lap.

Ned said, "When Marghie comes into the room it's as though a torch has been lit." He went to the sideboard to pour himself another glass of wine. "We wonder what's made our own such strangers to us. To adore them more than anything and get 'I hate you hate you hate you!' in response. You feel annihilated."

"We have our scenes from real life too," said Lilo. "We may have imposed too few or too many expectations. I haven't any idea which."

"But the point is, they're *here*, they're *with* you," Ned said, his voice getting husky.

Grisha said, "I remember asking my father once to tell me frankly if he'd ever wished that I'd not been born. And do you know, he said, 'Many times, briefly.' Young fool that I was, I held it against him. Until I realized that he had done his best, and done better than most."

"Impossible job," said Ned, crying freely again now, nodding.

Lilo said: "At the evening meal, our father routinely said to my brother, and not in jest, 'I wash my hands of you!' Later they would sit down to a game of pinochle. Eventually I understood that what Father was saying was, 'I *could* wash my hands of you!' "

"A god. He made and could unmake you," said Elise.

"Certainly Father *comported* himself as a god. I'm afraid what we called our love for him was really our fear."

"My own father was the mildest of men," Elise said. "It was Mother who was the divinity and the one to fear. If you were the daughter, at least. If you were the son you had a free pass."

Talking this way they could feel young, with only the link back in time, not yet the link forward. Exquisite to neglect for a moment the emotion of parenthood. "You're never carefree again," Ned said, "once you have *them* to sweat for." Just the momentary cessation of care, the momentary reprieve from the protean anxieties; it was not too much to claim.

Lilo said, "Why didn't it occur to us beforehand how frighteningly *original* they would be?"

"Yes," said Ned, "you can't be their author —"

"Unfortunately," put in Grisha.

"— you can only engender them, and stand back in bewilderment."

Elise said to Lilo, "What you call originality has gotten out of hand at our house."

A grimness went around with the coffee and dessert. Forks on plates and spoons on cups were too loud.

"Ah, but what is lovelier," asked Grisha, "than the noise of them storming around upstairs?" Lilo glared in disbelief.

"What on earth made you say such a thing?" she asked after the Dunallens had gone. He frankly didn't know. These days, uncharacteristically off-base or tactless remarks were popping out of him.

She washed the dishes. He dried. "It is my opinion," he said, "that Daniel and Gabriel are — are *very much in love*. Is there something we can do about it?"

"Nothing whatever."

"These are perhaps mistaken emotions."

"What do you suggest? That we send Gabriel away? Marghie is in love with him also. You've noticed?"

"Poor child. She is the mascot or sidekick or —"

"— third wheel, I'm afraid so. It's made her talkative. Too much the *entertainer*."

"That is a bit harsh, my dear. She cannot please you. As he cannot fail to."

Handing on the last dinner plate, she said, "The work of disciplining them has been mine not yours, Grisha." Studiously, he dried. "And you've not been present for most of it. Oh, it's *dry*, for God's sake!" She snatched the plate from him. "And I will not take *instruction* from you where the children are concerned." She awaited his rejoinder, and it worried her that Grisha, heretofore strong in a quarrel, looked back silently, overmatched.

———

Along about one — the house quiet, one light on at the head of the stairs — they returned on tiptoe, laughing. Danny and Gabriel leaned helplessly against the wall. Marghie put a hand over each mouth. What was so funny? Gabriel's impersonation of Peter Storrow. He hadn't much history in mimicry, was really just starting out, but Peter with his clerical demeanor and old-mannish distastes was too good to pass up. From him, miniature golf itself had come in for some pretty harsh strictures. Staring the while at Marg, Peter said he'd just watch. "Oh, you'll spoil it for *us* if you do!" she barked. "Pick up that club and get busy." Which he did; and after the first shot asked, Could he take it over? "Over? Over my dead body," she calmly said. At the third hole, after failing four times to get his ball past the whirling arms of the little windmill, he stormed off for a smoke. Marghie let out a pair of syllables that may have simply meant "spoilsport" in Hungarian but had a particular sense in the Hundert lexicon.

"*Rumlot* was our name," Danny said, "for this phantom little guy we blamed for any bad thing we ourselves had done. Means 'rotten.' 'Who left these roller skates on the stairs, may I ask?' 'Rotten.' He was our fall guy. This Rotten developed over time into a thief, first of things around the house, then of things in stores, where our life with him got more and more arbitrary."

"He'd advanced from Rotten to Putrid," said Marghie. "The store detectives at Carson Pirie Scott caught up with him. A certain Professor and Mrs. Hundert were telephoned."

"Oh boy," said Danny.

"After that Rotten was forced into early retirement."

"And died," said Danny.

Later, after tiptoeing across the hall to Danny's room, and tiptoeing back two hours later over floorboards that protested each step, Gabriel settled down to his diary:

The universal drive to SQUIRT, and the universal lassitude that follows.

Later. One night I picked up the sitting-room phone at exactly the same moment Dad picked up in his study, and a lady's voice said, "You gonna meet me, sweetheart?" and he said, in a hollow voice, "I am, yes." So hepped-up it never even occurred to him I might be listening. And then he told Mom some made-up thing, which he should have told the Marines, about a man from out of town he needed to talk to. And then he beat it out the door. Now I don't think that's open to very many interpretations.

Pious hypocrite! Stock figure! I've got a bone to pick with him, even if he is dead. And once I pick it, I'll be done. It'll slip my mind altogether that a man named Milton Geismar ever existed . . . Or else, no matter how long I live, he'll be the very last thing I think of. It seems all-important, at the intersection of time and eternity, to be thinking the

*right thought. Wish I could put in now for what it'll be. Just to be sure
nothing goes wrong. But what, if not that smoldering ogre, do I want
for my last thought? Oh, he'll be it.*

Marghie called them both to her room next morning, drew back
the curtain, pointed. Somebody had spelled out in gravel, on the
driveway, a declaration.

"Whoever wrote that," said Danny, "is going to have to be
clearer."

"It is," said Gabriel, "a cry for help."

"Who wrote that on the driveway?" called Lilo from the kitchen.

"Children, which of you has written this?" called Grisha from
the living room.

The theme of the day had emerged. "Don't anyone rub it out. I,
for one, am *moved*," Lilo said. "Someone in obscure distress wrote
that. Which of us was it?"

"I, for one, am creeped out," said Marghie. Had no one but herself
grasped that the optimal vantage point for reading this *cri de coeur*
in gravel was from her bedroom window? Clearly addressed to
her, the lovesick public notice read as follows:

I HAVE SUFFERED A WOUND TO MY FREE WILL!

Oh, go fuck yourself, she'd been inclined to reply. Go fuck
yourself, Peter Storrow. Where were the boys who knew how to
get beyond first person singular? She could count on one hand,
with digits to spare, the really worthwhile fellows, and they were
entwined with each other, gasping and sighing. Yes, she had put
an ear to the wall and listened. Then she had put a drinking glass
to the wall and an ear to that and heard Gabriel's pleas and her
brother's hedgings.

This summer, Wisconsin was rifer than usual with love and lovesickness. A perfect circle of unrequited emotion announced itself. Peter, it seemed, loved her, she loved Gabriel, Gabriel loved Danny, and Danny loved whom, what? The empty air. Compact all of himself, all self-delighting, no wonder everybody needed him — he seemed to need none of them.

What had lately occurred to Marghie was that love says "Satisfy! Satisfy!" and that what people really meant when they said, "I love you," is that they love the longed-for satisfaction of their need. People say "Love! Love!" and what they mean is "Me! Me!" If people loved each other the way they love themselves, people would love each other's need. It was not so, and that it was not so was quite a lot for a twenty-three-year-old virgin to bear.

It pleased her that without benefit of experience she'd thought her way in so deep. But she had to admit that Peter, also, seemed to have done some thinking. He'd suffered a wound to his free will. Well, that was a way of putting it, an interesting one. Could it be that for him too, gangrenous with desire though he was, sex had been thought about, not done? Could Peter Storrow be in like case? If she spelled out in gravel on the driveway, for all eyes but his heart only, something like

YOU A VIRGIN TOO?

they might strike up a very revealing correspondence.

Authoritative on affairs of the heart, despite having had none, she'd garnered what she knew from movies. From where else? Often enough, the television screen had sufficed despite crummy reception and commercial breaks. In *The Letter* or *Mildred Pierce* she had known pity and fear and purgation. Afterward, she'd turn off the set and try out a line or two she'd admired: "With all my heart, I still love the man I killed!" Or: "I learned the restaurant business, I learned it the hard way." This was what some called living vicariously. She called it living big, living at twenty-four frames per second. What was so great about real life anyhow? She'd been Greta Garbo, Hedy Lamar, Paulette Goddard, Myrna Loy, Ava Gardner. She had been Loretta Young, for what that was worth. She'd been Norma Shearer, a very classy experience. Marghie Hundert didn't so much watch movies as become them, didn't so much remember a picture as see it playing again, frame for frame, on the mind's eye. She had the conviction of the truly obsessed: none before her had felt so much. Now she drew another line from her storehouse and spoke it to herself: "Nothing between us but air, doll." And knew as she said it that this was a lie.

———

A box kite danced up and away from the meadow, with Ned at the other end. Gabriel waded into the high grass to join him.

"I tell myself that this is a form of work," said Ned. "I tell myself I'm teasing through something. Who knows but that I am? Where are the other young people?"

"Smoking. Bleeech."

"Ah, we've been trying to persuade Peter to quit. Does Marghie smoke?"

"She bummed one from Peter."

"Here's how old I am, Gabriel. I cannot get used to women smoking. I remember as a tiny boy, in the early nineteen-teens, waiting one afternoon to cross the railroad tracks. The train flew past and on the rear of the observation car I saw a woman smoking a cigarette and my mouth dropped open because I didn't know it was *physically* possible for women to smoke. I was close enough for her to see the expression on my face. She burst out laughing."

Ned and Elise and Grisha and Lilo had got nowhere trying to persuade any of the young to venture into Portage for an open-air production of *The Winter's Tale*. But Gabriel, on second thought, said he'd like to go. Danny said he wouldn't on a bet. Marghie seemed to have plans of some sort with, yes, Peter Storrow. All morning he'd shadowed her, darting from tree to tree. "Come out from there," she'd said, and they settled down to a smoke and rapid improvement of the acquaintance. Gabriel overheard them at midafternoon, chatting up a storm on the front porch. "We are no admirer of Jennifer Jones," she was saying.

The Dunallens' Volvo, a more trustworthy conveyance than the Hunderts' Studebaker, got the five of them to town. Gabriel kept quiet on the way, letting the crosstalk of the grown-ups go on as if he were not there. This *Winter's Tale* was an offering of the summer repertory company; bluntly, the local talent, green as peas. Ned said one had to admire the spunk of youngsters who'd tackle such a complex work. The audience in place, a weedy boy with a voice that had not securely changed stepped forth to say that the company would lead their audience from setting to setting. The play began at sunset, in a garden adjacent to the public library. This was Sicily. Then on to the seacoast of Bohemia, which was a vacant lot down the block, lit by campfires. Final destination was the First Methodist Church, aglow with several hundred candles. This was Paulina's chapel. The Wisconsin accents of the cast were uniformly strong. The company couldn't afford a whole bear, just a bear paw, waved menacingly at the crowd. Had they bitten off more than they could chew, these players? Leontes's tights were meant for a larger man. Polixenes had a tendency to lapse out of character when not speaking his lines. Hermione was wide in the beam. Florizel had only a head of golden curls to see him through. But there was a composed and shining Perdita who was what Perdita should be, renewal out of time's wastes. And when, by firelight, she spoke of Great Creating Nature, the words were a clarion and the crowd forgot to breathe. Ned wasn't crying for once, he was exulting. He was lightning in a bottle, he was the red blood reigning. Gabriel cast a sidelong reverent look that said, in all but words, *You cut your throat for love, Ned Dunallen.*

PART TWO

PART TWO

three

SEEING STARS

Chicago, autumn, 1974. Gabriel hung on the wall of spartan quarters at International House a picture of his current hero, Edwin Hubble, whose identification of the nebulae as distant galaxies, not gaseous clouds, increased the known universe by a factor of a thousand million; whose mathematical constant established that one hundred billion trillion stars race away from us more swiftly in direct proportion as they are more distant; who proved that the expanding universe is the same in all directions, homogeneous as far as the mind can see. Gabriel had received graduate-school offers from Cambridge and Cal Tech and Princeton among others, but settled on the University of Chicago after Grisha urged him to make his future there. "Choose your speciality, settle down to it, and flourish to your capacities. Here is where the immortal things will happen in astrophysics, I prophesy, science I shall not live to see but you, my boy, may take a wigorous hand in."

The moment of creation, and how the universe went from smooth to lumpy — that seemed sufficiently interesting. Also supernovae, from whose dust all elements heavier than lithium derive; the quantum mechanics of black holes; the dark or missing ninety-five to ninety-nine percent of matter; above all, though it was considered a (literally) unutterable topic, what there was before (so to speak) the creation of space-time in the Big Bang. Here Gabriel presumed to have a prescientific hunch, kept strictly to himself. It was simultaneously dawning on the three or four best cosmological minds: the multiverse, universes budding from one another, a profusion of universes without beginning or end, our own the merest upstart in the myriad. Universes without beginning or end — this bright idea, with its reintroduction of eternity, infinite regress and infinite progress, universes forever abounding, whispered to Gabriel that perhaps he hadn't come so far from Terpsichore Street after all since, soberly considered, he was only putting eternal Nature where the eternal God of Abraham, Isaac, and Jacob used to be.

Marghie wasn't much on the cosmos. She'd listen politely while Gabriel went on about quasars and supernovae and neutron stars and the rest. She had stars of her own, honored at The Lampion, her establishment on Division. It had been, in the long ago, a little unbalconied vaudeville house called Feingold's, then a haggard burlesque house called The Blue Dahlia, then nothing and in bad shape for years. She combined a small business loan with the boon of a modest investment by her parents and reincarnated the place as an art house specializing in the most serious of serious European films and the most seriously entertaining of American movies. You got nowhere talking to her about any real world. Read a newspaper? Only if it were to say "Dictators Resign in Droves" or "Cancer Extinct as the Dodo" or "Jews and Arabs in Love Fest" or "Everything Fine, Thank God, in Africa." She liked her Nazis as Lubitsch portrayed them in *To Be or Not to Be*, outwitted and sent packing by Carole Lombard and Jack Benny, no match for their comic timing. What she knew about China was from Sternberg's *Shanghai Express*. "You haven't seen it? Dietrich is this much-handled parcel of goods. Very gorgeous in black feathers. 'It took more than one man to change my name to Shanghai Lily,' she says. And she can't decide whether she only cares about herself or she's a diva of self-sacrifice and high purpose. That's Marlene's way. You've really never seen it? . . . Then which Dietrich *have* you seen? . . . *What?* Well, when you do, here's what to watch for, her open secret, observable in every frame. *She's ludicrous!* I mean this in the nicest way. I mean she's so convinced in her ludicrousness that it's catching. You start putting your own hand on your hip in that haughty style of hers. It's narcissism all right, but what's so wrong when it's big-tent narcissism and everybody's welcome?" Sternberg's *Shanghai Gesture* — in which Gene Tierney, an addict of the chemin de-fer tables, degenerates into a wild animal in an evening gown — was the rest of what she knew about China. What she knew about adultery was *Back Street*. "The second *Back Street*. The first is an indifferent business with Irene Dunne. The third, with Susan Hayward, is beneath discussion. The second's the one, with Maggie Sullavan." Sternberg's *Morocco*, in which Dietrich has her choice between Gary Cooper and Adolphe Menjou, was what she knew about Morocco. Cooper or Menjou — not a dead heat in anybody's heart, but Marlene leads Adolphe a chase before walking into the Sahara, barefoot and head high, to follow in the rear guard of Gary's detachment of the Foreign Legion.

"Don't tell me you've never *seen* it! Dietrich's a café singer, she's come *way* down in the world. Playing some two-bit club. Well, Gary comes up to her room and he's no gentleman, and no gentleman's what she's looking for. He asks what a girl like her is doing in joint like that, and she says, 'I understand that men are never asked why they entered the Legion.' So Gary says, 'When I crashed the Legion, I ditched the past.' So she blows some smoke at him and says, very slowly and deliberately, 'There's a Foreign Legion of women too. But we have no uniforms, no flag, and no medals. No wound stripes when we are hurt. Yet we are brave.' " Marghie started the first reel of this evening's feature and they took their seats in the last row, under the wavering light. Here was their favorite thing, to watch a movie, only the two of them, after the doors were locked and the little marquee darkened.

She was down in the dumps tonight. Very modest box office all week. Her Margaret Sullavan festival had not been a success. *The*

Shining Hour, So Ends Our Night, The Shop Around the Corner, No Sad Songs for Me, Three Comrades, Next Time We Love, The Mortal Storm, Little Man, What Now? and, of course, *Back Street.* It was mainly old biddies who came to watch Maggie gain by a whisker or lose forever life's reward. Her voice had a burr on it, by the sound of which you knew the odds on a happy ending were long. The biddies loved her. "Very well then," said Marghie. "Count me among the biddies." This evening's feature was something else again — *Dodsworth.* Gabriel hadn't seen it. Marghie glared in disbelief. The credits rolled. Into her lap leapt Louise and into Gabriel's Baby June, cats named to honor the old days of Feingold's and The Blue Dahlia, good mousers, fine girls. "In the Hall of Fame of Cats," Marghie liked to say.

Gabriel admired how, as the situation developed in a film, she'd talk about the characters as if they were real people. "Got the perfect man and doesn't know it," she said tonight of Ruth Chatterton in the role of Mrs. Dodsworth. "Running after glorified lounge lizards!" (David Niven and Paul Lukas.) Then comes the crisis when Fran Dodsworth falls for a transparent Austrian fortune hunter, young and slickly handsome and titled but very poor "seeence zeee var," and he brings his country frump of a mother, played by Maria Ouspenskaya, to meet this woman older by years than she pretends, and the battle-ax sizes her up and says, "Have you thought, my dear, how little happiness there can be for the *old* wife of a *young* husband?"

"Serves you *right!*" Marghie hollered at the screen. Her praise was all for Mrs. Cortright, the expatriate "other woman" in Dodsworth's affections, played by Mary Astor. "The *noble* Mary Astor. If I could carry it off, I'd be like her. Noble, as you see, but not icky noble, not Greer Garson." She declared *Dodsworth* Wyler's best, bar none. (Presiding creed at this theater was *auteurisme,* needless to say.) "How'd you like it?"

"Liked it fine." But with that Baby June, who'd let herself be stroked throughout the movie, turned and scratched him.

"Son of a bitch!"

"Her gender, Gabriel, is female. Her genus is cat. She cannot be a *son* of a *bitch*. Draw blood?"

"A little. I tell you what, Marg, I prefer dogs. Dogs aren't so —"

"Perfidious?"

"Perfidious."

"Dogs were domesticated a hundred thirty thousand years ago. Cats were domesticated in 1957. Oh, June's feisty, I admit. You ought to see her at the vet's. One look at that rectal thermometer and she starts to spit and yowl. They have to use the steel-mesh gloves to hold her. Never necessary with Louise, great lady that she is. Louise just closes her eyes and thinks of England." She doled out a can of wet food for the girls and replenished their water. "Watch 'em go for it. I've never seen such cats. They eat like you-know-whats, starts with *d*. And they *eliminate* like guys."

On account of Earth Shoes, Marghie tilted backward nowadays. She stood awhile stroking the one big braid she currently wore, then checked the doors and turned out the lights. They decided on a walk down State and onto Walton, past the Scottish Rite, then diagonally through Bughouse Square. Gabriel was reporting on his fellow graduate students, who among them was a genius and who was not. "There's this horse's ass, Ross Something or Something Ross, out of his depth and driven crazy, I guess, after being publicly humiliated by Lustig, who told him he was wasting our time with secondary-school truisms. Rumor is, the guy had a little gift-wrapped package sent over to Lustig's house. A rat nailed to a board. Not yet out of its misery. News like that gets around an astronomy department pretty fast. What time is it? Oh, God, I'm due at his lecture on white dwarfs at seven."

"In the morning? Lustig lectures at seven in the morning? He deserves a rat nailed to a board. I'll drag myself out of bed at noon if I'm lucky. How do you manage on so little sleep?"

"Naps. I take six a day, as Buckminster Fuller recommends. It really works, at least for a while. Then you collapse. I took two naps during that movie and you didn't even notice."

Old Town was strung with Christmas lights. A dry steady snow had muffled up the neighborhood. Gabriel was hungry, as always. He suggested an all-night Mexican place at Clark at Erie. Marghie made a face of death, and off they went.

On the way, she lapsed into a scene from *Leave Her to Heaven*, starring Gene Tierney, due for a one-night run next week. The monstrously beautiful Tierney was a particular passion of Marg's. "She plays this black widow, very rich, houses everywhere. And Cornel Wilde falls for her. Not her money, just her. He's a very high-minded humanitarian type who's traveled all around the world to look at poor people, and while the two of them are lounging around one of her gorgeous houses he gets wrought up and says, 'Ellen, Ellen, do you know what it is to be truly hungry?' and she says, 'I'm hungry right now!'"

"Me too." They came to Clark and Erie.

"The only thing I like here is that challenge over the bar," she said when they entered.

FREE CAR WITH PURCHASE OF 1,000,000,000 TACOS!

"I'd like to own that sign. I'd like to have it in my kitchen." Gabriel placed his order. "A number two, please, but with extra sauce and scallions and no cheese. Better yet, could I have the sauce that goes on number eight instead of the number-two sauce?"

"You always order something that's not on the menu. Gabriel, are you like that in bed? Give me a Tab, please," she said to the waitress, "and just the way it comes from the bottling plant will be fine."

Gabriel ate his customized taco. Marghie sipped her Tab. "Lustig gets on my nerves," he said. "Every time you try to tell him something, he says, 'I know.' I cannot utter any declarative sentence without Lustig saying he knows. So I told him I wear briefs not boxers, just to see what would happen."

"You did not."

"Okay, okay." He chewed a while. Delicious taco. "How's lover boy?"

"I'll thank you to call him by his Christian name."

"We can agree that he's that, anyhow. How's Peter?"

"Writes me several times a day. Calls every night."

"How come you two don't see each other more often?"

"We've got our arrangement. He comes here once in a while. I go there once in a very great while. He's busy, you know. He's writing the *definitive* study of the Cliff Dwellers —"

"Wonder how he came up with them."

"— and needs absolute concentration."

Gabriel chewed heartily, looked reflective. She couldn't make out whether he was thinking about Peter or about what he was eating. He said, "I've been doing a little —"

"Don't talk with your mouth full. You take too-big bites."

He chewed, swallowed. "A little dating myself."

"You? Tell all."

"First was Scott. Jewish boy from Toronto, every hair in place, perfect clothes, and so we got to talking and he steered the conversation to his favorite topic, housework. I'd think we were safely on to something else, but no, we'd suddenly be back to the perils of mold and like that. I got to know him pretty well over the course of a weekend, well enough to know he was in the grip of an obsessive-compulsive disorder. We came to grief when I said so. Next was Skip. Said his real name was Eugene, but nobody calls him that except the police. Then there was this other one. Real

nice, a Russian Jew — uncircumcised, what do you think of that?
— who told me about all of his erotic adventures in the Soviet
Union. Said he'd had sex for first time under Khrushchev. Then
there was this redhead, big freckles all over him, cornflower-blue
eyes, something to see."

"I do like redheads."

"Me too. His name was Blair or Todd or one of those names.
Anyhow, he told me that the day their father died he and his little
brother had sex. Said it happened just like that, without a word
between them. And that it had happened only that once, and that
they'd never in all these years talked about it, but that his brother
was the only one he'd ever love. He told me all this after knowing
me for only a few minutes, so I wonder if he just automatically
tells everybody. Then I ran into him a few weeks later and he was
reproachful with me, as if I'd wronged him. I saw him one more
time after that and he snubbed me altogether. So here I am with
this extremely private piece of information I don't really want. If it
were the sort of thing you could give back, I would."

"I have a question."

"What?"

"These redheads, are they red all over?"

"You mean, are they *pubically* red?"

"Yes."

"I believe so. One night I was walking along Roscoe when this
other fellow, a brunette, not a redhead, walked up and said, 'Will
you marry me?' I've been thinking, ever since, what if I'd just said
yes? What would that life have been? I mean, assuming he was
serious."

"Quite a large assumption."

"Yes, but *if*. Maybe I walked away from life's sweetest
opportunity."

"Maybe you'll run into him again."

"I'll never."

"Because you just now made him up."

"Right."

Ebb tide. When all the other topics had run out, when he was done talking about his stars and she about hers, about his ordering habits in Chicago's restaurants, about the redhead and the Russian and the rest, Marghie and Gabriel would fall silent and there Danny — the now *famous* Daniel Hundert of Hyde Park, Illinois — would be between them. *Time* and *Newsweek* had made his story known to the nation, as had Huntley and Brinkley. True, Howard K. Smith broadcast a disparaging commentary; but Sevareid countered with a favorable one. "Good old Eric Clarified," said Marghie. "Knew we could count on him."

For ten days before and after Christmas of 1972, flush with his epic electoral triumph, Richard Nixon had dropped more ordnance on Hanoi and Haiphong than fell on Japan in all of World War II. On the night of December 22, for the second time, bombs struck Bach Mai Hospital in the capital, killing two hundred and eighty sick people in their beds.

"I'm not," Danny said, "saying another word till this is all over." He'd declared again and again that he would rather go to Canada than serve, although a high draft number made the matter moot. Originally, what he'd launched into was a hunger strike, but after skipping only the third meal found himself feeding inconsolably in front of the open refrigerator. No, a silence not a hunger artist was what he would be. By the rigors of such a testing, Danny had come into his own.

"I went down for dinner last week," Marghie said. "Mom's very patient with him. He does things around the house, you know — cleans, does laundry. He's sweet. Kisses everybody, kisses Dad, too. Kisses the doorman. People in the building have read about him. They look condolingly at Mom and Dad. In the elevator one day, somebody from the Sociology Department pumped Danny's hand and said how magnificent it all was and that the name of Daniel Hundert was universally known among antiwar activists and that his many months of refusing to speak might well be the loudest and most memorable cry against our criminal presence in Southeast Asia and so on. Did I tell you Wayne Morse read him into the Congressional Record? Mom writes letters to what's-his-name, old unforgettable, oh, what the hell's his name, saying, 'My son begs you, Mr. President, by his silence, to end this horror. He will not speak until the last American personnel have left Vietnam.' Ford, Gerald Ford. And some underskinker responds."

This silence, strictly kept up for almost two years now, surrounded Danny like an element. He lived with his parents at the Powhatan, on Fiftieth Street, in what had always been his bedroom, volunteered for work he could carry out mutely at a nearby center for the indigent, and haunted Regenstein Library, reading all he could about the long overlording of a very ancient civilization — by the Chinese for a thousand years, by the French and Japanese and French, and now the Americans. He read how in 1919 at Versailles, inspired by Woodrow Wilson's fourteen points calling for national self-determination, Nguyen Ai Quoc — "Nguyen the Patriot" — and his ragtag of followers had attempted to present the conference with a proposal calling for their own freedom. (Turned away.) About Nguyen's formation in 1941 of the Vietnam Independence League or Viet Minh, a united popular front, Communist-led, of all Vietnamese nationalists. About how after thirteen months as a prisoner of Chiang Kai-shek in Peking, Nguyen comes back to Vietnam bearing the battle name of Ho Chi Minh — "Ho the Enlightened One," and once the defeated Japanese withdraw begins a letter-writing campaign to President Truman asking for American assistance in gaining Vietnam's independence from France. (No reply.) About how in 1945 Ho Chi

Minh, quoting from the American Declaration of Independence, proclaims the Independent Democratic Republic of Vietnam, and about how General Jacques-Philippe Leclerc, France's military commander in Indochina, arrives at Saigon declaring: "We are here to reclaim our inheritance."

This particular bit of colonialist temerity brought Danny to his feet, sent him prowling the stacks of Regenstein. The background to specifically American crimes against Southeast Asia, previously a blur, he saw now with wild-making clarity. True, he appeared at a glance to be like any other of those botch-ups seen along the Midway Plaisance — learned misfits hopped up on their wrath, with all but the dissertation and all but a clue as to how to get on in the world; ideologized washouts hot to the breaking point to proclaim things that universal common sense already acknowledges or that universal common sense will never remotely entertain; *Luftmenschen* shading away to the seriously insane. But unlike them he'd grown substantial, public even, belonged now to the evening news, forecourt of history itself.

Back at his favorite carrel, on two, at the rear of the study lounge, he read about President Eisenhower justifying the French defense of a garrison at Dien Bien Phu: "You have a row of dominoes set up, and you knock over the first one, and what will happen to the last one is the certainty that it will go over very quickly." About the fall of Dien Bien Phu and with it the end of France's delusion that it could dominate in Asia. (Alas, poor America, so slow to find out what General Giap had demonstrated with Gallic clarity to General Navarre on the seventh of May 1954 in a valley in Tonkin.) The partition of Vietnam at the seventeenth parallel followed, decreed at Geneva, along with the promise of an election in two years and, after that, reunification. Wagging the thumb and index finger, Vietnamese would greet each other with an optimistic "In two years!" Forlorn hope. In the rigged election of October 23, 1955, conducted ahead of schedule and only in the south, Ngo Dinh Diem receives more than ninety-eight percent of the vote. (In Saigon the number of votes for Diem exceeds by one third the total number of registered voters.) He proclaims the Republic of South Vietnam and himself as its first president. He appoints himself prime minister, minister of defense, and supreme commander of the armed forces . . .

At eleven thirty the first bell rang. At eleven forty-five the second. Library closing, time to go.

Daniel Hundert's quietude in such a talkative land had something like the moral authority of a monk on fire in Vietnam. The evening staff at Regenstein, most of them work-study undergraduates, treated him with respect. The prestige of weirdness went before Danny. Many knew his story. Those who did not assumed him to be deaf and mute, as he only ever smiled, or groaned in the depths of his throat. One evening, a nasty pre-med sneaked up from behind and clapped his hands together at ear-level. Danny turned around in a pantomime of rage wild enough to scare the kid. Typically, though, he'd be left to his labors. He scoured books, newspapers, periodicals, mastering in detail the new American story that repeated in its bitter essentials the old French one. He read about the arrival at Da Nang in 1965 of the first U.S. combat units, about General Westmoreland's announcement in 1967 that "the enemy's hopes are bankrupt," about the North Vietnamese siege of Khe Sanh, about the Plain of Jars, Hamburger Hill, My Lai.

He undertook to memorize the names and hometowns of the dead that he might build a mnemonic monument to the more than fifty thousand squandered Americans. His mind grew into a welter of dead boys' names, along with those of their mothers and fathers and siblings and wives and babies. All of this he earnestly tried to hold in his head, for he despaired of any monument less than complete. Indeed, what he really longed for was a vast unbuildable addition — it would have cleft open his brain — to house in memory unlearnable names of the more than two million Vietnamese who'd perished.

On the evening of February 5, 1973, six weeks into his protest, he watched on the evening news as Colonel William Nolde, the 57,597th — and last — American soldier to die in combat in Vietnam was laid to rest at Arlington National Cemetery.

"I've forgotten what you sound like," Lilo said to her son. "It's over. They're out now."

"So pipe up," said Marghie.

As for the professor, he said little, seeming preoccupied, or waylaid, or stymied. A half-absence Lilo had never seen before encroached on him. One day he'd angered her by saying, "Which war?" Other people's children were fire-bombing ROTC buildings, when not setting off devices accidentally in the basements of Greenwich Village townhouses, or being shot dead by National Guardsmen. A very compliant, sweet-natured, utterly dependent little boy was what their Daniel had become. They sent him to psychiatrists, of course, who prescribed ever-stronger medicines, culminating in lithium, none of which had the slightest effect. Suspecting he was flushing his pills down the toilet, Lilo made him take them in front of her. Even so, she wondered, was he hiding the dose under his tongue, despite downing full glasses of water? To search his mouth was an indignity she could not bring herself to inflict. "He's not crazy, Mom," said Marghie. "He's angry. He's executing his plan, making his case." Her boy was safe inside his protest, Lilo told or tried to tell herself, and one day would come out again. Mothers had known worse, to put it mildly.

But Danny did not pipe up once the American deaths ended. He had said till the last personnel were out, and evidently meant it. Peace talks underway? Thousands of Americans, and tens of thousands of Vietnamese, had died while in a Parisian villa diplomats settled nothing more momentous than the shape of the conference table. Danny hewed to silence. The certainty had got into him that he could stop this infamy. But the "Vietnamized" war ground on still. By now the Great Trickster had left the stage. A man as empty of inner torment as his predecessor had been full of it, a not at all Shakespearean man, a nonentity of a man, had ascended to the White House. Danny cleaved to silence.

"I saw him the other day," Gabriel said. "He was walking west on Woodlawn and I was walking east. He didn't exactly ignore me. He gave me a secret smile, the kind spies must use. But then he looked away, and pulled his scarf tighter and cap lower and hurried off. I got a sick feeling."

"What was it you two fought about?"

"Something little. Some fight about nothing that he picked and I pitched into. Afterward he sent me a letter. And it was blank. Just an empty sheet of paper put in an envelope and mailed. A few days later he stopped talking to everybody else. I'm proud to *claim priority*, as we scientists say. He cut the lines to me first."

"You should see how many letters he's had, most of them nice."

"He certainly is the fair-haired boy, of something. Got that capable look in his eye."

"Capable of anything. I know him."

"So do I."

"*I* know what he's going to do before he does it. Sometimes, anyhow." This from a girl who deplored oracles, auguries, and the like, who howled at astrology, crystal gazing, the planchette. "I knew, when we were eight, one summer in Wisconsin, that he was going to roll up the windows of Mom and Dad's car, all except for one just a little bit, and stick a garden hose in and, well, you can imagine. Not the current Studebaker, the one before. He didn't want them to go out that night. Did he tell me he was going to do it? No. But I knew. And I always knew when he was going to shoplift something. Nothing very big ever. Just little things, to show he could. And I always knew when he was going to run away. And you know what, Gabriel? I knew beforehand, way beforehand, that he was going to fuck you."

"That nobody would have needed second sight for."

"Second sight? Phooey! Not what I'm talking about. You know I don't believe in such things. I do believe in *twinship* though, especially this underrated fraternal kind. We're in nearly constant communion, Danny and I. And what I know is that this silence is refining him, cleansing him. But for the better? I liked my brother when he was a big contradictory mess. I'm afraid he's arrived now at some kind of purity."

"Purity's all right."

"No. I mean the purity of one idea."

"What idea?"

"Don't know."

"Constant communion, you said, Marg."

"I believe 'nearly constant' is what I said."

They ambled along, enjoying each other's silence, breaths rising on the air, and came now to the train station. Gabriel threw his head back and produced a semblance of smoke rings, quickly gone. "Oh, I forgot to tell you something."

"What's that?"

"I got on a bus this morning."

"Yes?"

"And the bus got pulled over."

"Pulled over by a cop?"

"Yes, by a cop. Have you ever heard of such a thing? And this cop came on the bus, and he gave the driver a ticket."

"Really?"

"And then he gave everybody else a ticket too."

"Really?"

"Even the little babies got tickets."

"Oh, you're lying, *lying*!" she raged. "Why do I fall for these absurdities?"

"Don't know, Marg, but sometimes you do." Snow was accumulating on their shoulders and caps. A draft of steam went up from Gabriel's mouth. "Get even with me sometime, if you can." The last train was pulling into the station. He dashed for it, recalling as he went how his parents would say so often that they'd wanted a little sister for him, and tried so hard to make one, but no such luck and that instead they were giving all their love to him. And so he had gone out into the wilderness to find a sister, and lo, here she was. A little sister? What good would that be? A big sister was much better, a big sister was the ticket.

"Hope you eat a rug!" Marghie called down to the platform.

"Hope you drink lye!" he called back.

"Hope you get run over by a boat!"

"Hope you catch fire!"

Thus they loved.

———

At the Powhatan, a spare room giving onto an airshaft, referred to only as "the spare room," was in practice Lilo's study. A typewriter, a gooseneck lamp, a tiny desk, two chairs, and row on row of books. She was a scholar on her own time, one of those wives common to her generation who'd given up all professional claims, the better to serve as helpmeet. Her work in progress — immemorially in progress and a matter for eye-rolling between the twins — had been something Gabriel didn't inquire into till, one afternoon that winter, sitting with him over tea in the spare room, she said what she was writing: a history of the Gypsies.

"Tell me. I don't know the first thing."

"Sometime before the ninth century they left —"

"India."

"Yes, dear, India. Why they left, and when, and in what phases — these things are harder to know. At any rate, they went to Persia, where they picked up new genes and where their language underwent certain changes. After that, all through the Balkans and into Bohemia and onward as far as Spain and England. In the process they became something new, a European people, even if a most unusual one."

"They didn't marry strictly among themselves?"

"Oh, there is no 'strictly' in such matters. One of the results of any diaspora is new genes coming in. People on islands, people hemmed in by mountains, may sometimes, for certain periods, be strictly endogamous. But people on the road, no."

"None went back?"

"To India? They promptly forgot that they had come from India. It was assumed that they'd come from Egypt, and words like 'Zigeuner' and 'Gitano' and 'Gypsy' are modifications of 'Egyptian.' But the Gypsies call themselves 'Roma' and 'Sinti.' Or they call themselves Travelers, even when they've settled down. As for religion, they had none of their own. When God was handing out the religions, the Gypsies wrote theirs down on a cabbage leaf and a donkey ate it. Or so they like to say. They've followed the religion of wherever they've found themselves — Muslim among Muslims, Catholic among Catholics, Protestant among Protestants, Orthodox among Orthodox. Not that it has kept them from being hunted for sport, or else enslaved."

"Hard to believe they just forgot where they'd come from. They sound like the opposite of the Jews."

"In some ways, yes. A people without priests, without written language or sacred texts, without a codified history or a duty to remember the dead."

"How have they made out?"

"Less well than the Jews."

"I know somebody who used to make fun of me for sizing up everything vis-à-vis the Jews. Said I was parochial."

"My son, by any chance?"

"He told you? About how it drove him crazy?"

"Back when. Not at all unkindly."

A long beat while Gabriel wondered what else he'd told. "You know why I harp on the Jews, Lilo? A last little tip of the hat to Zion, and then, goodbye, O Zion, and good —"

"No, my dear, the riddance doesn't come so easily. Wanting not to be Jewish is itself Jewish, don't you see? You'd have to turn into somebody else altogether. You'd have to become as forgetful as a Gypsy not to be Jewish anymore."

It came back to him, that conversation, a few months later in Portage. Grisha was explaining, while he put the forty-five on the turntable, "She has thrown into the fire the wrong baby." *Il Trovatore*, a 1930s recording on ten discs. Grisha and Lilo didn't say "stereo" or even "phonograph" or "record player." "Victrola" was the word, and the appliance here was old enough to wear the name very comfortably. From the needle came a growling and popping; voices stirred. Grisha sank down in his regular chair. He listened hard, smiled.

"Immediacy of attack is what I love in him. And miss utterly in that other one, that German whose name is not spoken in our house. Do you know this, Gabriel?" Gabriel knew no operas whatsoever. Grisha did what he could to boil down *Trovatore*. "Many years ago, because overwrought, the Gypsy woman, whose name escapes me —"

Here they were again, the Gypsies. The more deeply he entered into Hundertdom, the more Gabriel was hearing about Gypsies. They were somehow the red thread woven through.

"Azucena, dear," Lilo called from the kitchen.

"Azucena has thrown the wrong baby, her own, into the fire,

et cetera. The Count di Luna is mortally jealous of a mysterious troubadour, whose name escapes me —"

"Manrico," Lilo called.

"— Manrico, son of, of —"

"Azucena," she called.

"— Azucena."

"Or maybe not!"

"Or maybe not; she is right about this. Manrico, who either is or is not the son of Azucena, sings each night in the palace garden. There is a civil war in progress. The place is northern Spain, the fifteenth century and so on, to the uttermost extremes of absurdity and confusion. You will like it."

Lilo had gone fishing that day with a view to dinner. She rowed her dinghy out for yellow perch and common pike. A handsome three- to four-pound example of the latter was what she'd poached in a court bouillon: she'd skinned it, she'd made an aspic of the bouillon, she'd mixed this with a mayonnaise and masked the pike. She'd chilled till set. The worse the developing torments around her, the more ardent was Lilo in the kitchen.

"Dear, that's the best synopsis ever of *Trovatore*. Better than Milton Cross could do." She was bearing to the table the pike with its garnish of *salade russe*, cucumber, and eggs with pimento. "We used to listen every Saturday," she said to Gabriel.

"Texaco presents!" said the old man, eyes shut. He tended more and more to shut his eyes when speaking.

"There was this Milton Cross fellow. His synopses were very muddy," Lilo said.

"And then one Saturday poor Cross's wife had died," Grisha continued, "and there had to be a, how do you say, a stand-in. It was, I believe, the only time the United States ever understood the plot to an opera." Thus any good story got divvied up. The shank end was Grisha's to tell.

"Who brightens the life of the gypsy? *The gypsy maiden!*" sang La Scala's chorus to a clangor of hammers on anvils. Here Grisha gave Gabriel what looked maybe like a confidential wink of the eye, then shut off *Trovatore*. They ate Lilo's pike. The fiery day settled into evening, not Louisiana-close but sticky enough. Cold-fish supper had been an inspiration.

No wine was offered, unusual at this table. They'd drunk only seltzer water with the meal. No drink before dinner either. But, "We have a little wine for our dessert," Lilo now said, bringing in a dark green bottle from the kitchen and setting it before Grisha.

He put on his half-lenses, examined the label in a leisurely way. "We have here the supremacy of all sweet wines." He uncorked the Tokaj Essencia, poured three glassfuls. "You have tried Sauternes? They are kerosene. Forget them." The glowing beverage behaved like a medicine, Gabriel observed, rolling it around in his glass.

"*Egeszségédre!*" Lilo said, raising hers.

"*Egeszségédre!*" echoed Grisha, and savored the first taste. "Oh, it is merely what the tsars drank upon their deathbeds. To make certain they would return. As ghosts, inwisibly presiding." He sipped. "Hits the spot!" He'd been, in his time, a great aficionado of such Americanisms, claimed to have read all three volumes of Mencken's *The American Language: An Inquiry Into the Development of English in the United States*. In his bloodthirsty accent he'd refer to some film star as a very tasty dish, his automobile as a flivver, those mortally ill as goners. He'd speak of a lead-pipe cinch, say okey-dokey when he meant fine, beeswax when he meant business. His mind he referred to as the hopper.

"Delicious," said Gabriel.

"Entirely from the noble rot." What was he talking about? Strange lore of the oenophile. Although the bottle was not within reach, Gabriel irrationally began to fear he might somehow upset this elixir worthy of a dying emperor, this noble rot. "Maybe too rich for my blood."

"For anybody's," said Lilo. She sipped, marveled, sipped again. "Raisins, plums, and . . ."

"And the least droplet of armsweat," Grisha said.

"And a hint of baked apple."

"No, of baked pear."

"And underneath all that, something geologic, some taste of —"

"Wolcano."

"Precisely."

Now all fell silent at the bark of a fox nearby. Fleeing it, who should bound in through an unscreened window but Franush, the tortoiseshell cat who'd adopted them here last summer. Talk about a Hall of Famer! Back in Chicago Lilo had resorted to a water pistol to try to keep him off the table. You wondered why she bothered; it didn't work. He arched his back Halloween-style — a cat not to be patronized or even looked at, evidently, for like God upon Sinai, consenting to be seen only from behind, Franush turned on his heel, glared with his anus, strode away.

"A too-brief appearance, Franush!" called Lilo.

"On account of Franush," Grisha said, "wery little wildlife surwives in Wisconsin. The perfect gentleman at Hyde Park — up here, a death squad. He arrives after months of confinement and reclaims his rights according to nature. We would not interfere for the world."

"I feed him and feed him," Lilo said. "Still he brings home moles, voles, mice, chipmunks, little rabbits. I hate having to take sides against Franush. But I did when he got a loon, a fledgling."

"This was the wery worst," said Grisha, and then out of him came an inhuman screech. "Exactly what we heard all night. The inconsolable mother loon." He went over to the Victrola, put *Trovatore* back on.

Gabriel helped Lilo to clear the table. In the kitchen, she put on the kettle for tea. He rinsed the dishes.

"I liked that nice young man you brought around to dinner during the spring term. Will we see him again?"

"Doubt it. I liked him too. He must have made up his mind he didn't like me."

"There will be others."

"No, Lilo. I'm all done with that. The last one I went out with was so boring he told me all the contents of his refrigerator. The one before that remembered something else he had to do fifteen minutes into the date. The one before that had to cancel because his older brother had shot somebody that afternoon. The one before that said nothing could compare to having been head cheerleader at New Trier High. The one before that told me if I believe men walked on the moon I must be a sucker, because it was nothing but a hoax. The one before that was sweet, a kid from Kentucky who said he sure was looking for a power mower — *paramour*, he meant; and, Lilo, I sure was ready for the job, but didn't get the offer. The one before that lightened me of my wristwatch and wallet. The one before that —"

"You frighten me with these stories."

"I lose all hope, then I get it back. This is no plus," he said, holding up the Siamese thumbs. "Or maybe it's just my excuse. The other day I saw an ad in the personals I was tempted to answer. 'Looking for someone handsomer than Joel McCrae, richer than Howard Hughes, wiser than the Buddha.' What do you think the guy is like who wrote that?"

Silence.

"Maybe I'll drop him a line." He cupped his hands to the window and peered in the direction of the Dunallens' house. All was dark. "Where are Ned and Ellie?"

"Off to Seattle for a few weeks. Ellie's old father is ailing. Ninety-seven, and was hale and hearty till just this year. Think of it." Again the howl of a fox brought them up short. Then another, quite different, farther off. It was call and response, it was love, which between foxes sounds the same as despair.

A couple of months ago, Lilo and Marghie had sat Danny down in front of the television to see the last Americans helicoptered from the roof of the embassy in Saigon. "The *very* last, see?" Marghie had said, splaying a hand at the television. He gave his head a shake that meant — nothing doing. He would keep silent, keep the faith of his calling.

"Does Marghie —" There were troubles proliferating on every hand, too peremptory not to speak about. "Have you told Marghie about Grisha?"

"She's driving up tomorrow. I will tell her then."

"Marghie? Tomorrow?"

"She hadn't wanted you to know she was coming up. Do please feign surprise when you see her." She poured. They drank. In a ruined hut, beside a mountain in Biscay, the Gypsies in the next room sang loud enough for Lilo to say to Gabriel, in a low tone, "He put on his hat and wandered off the other day. I found him on the road a mile from here. When I said, 'Where do you think you're going?' he shrugged. He didn't know. There's more and more he doesn't know. One day he's himself, the next all disconnection. He'll say to me 'That person' or 'that thing' or just, 'You know, you know.' I say, 'No, I don't know.' Then likely as not he'll lash out. He has accused me of trying to trick him, and of stealing from him." She swallowed hard, firm against tears. "He has called me abominable names. In between times, yes, he is fine. So long as the past is under discussion, I've noticed, he seems well enough. There's a performance that goes on, a mimicry of normal life. Tonight was good, yes. But I see his exhaustion from trying, for other people's sake, to impersonate himself. You will too. He'll not be able to keep it up. He hasn't two good days in a row anymore."

Crescendo from the next room, then silence, only the finished side saying *tsk, tsk.* "As for the music, it has become his hiding place." She cocked an ear. "Asleep, I expect. A little wine puts him out now."

"He's seen a doctor?"

"Oh, yes, a young neurologist who told us about the biology of memory, as he called it. Hippocampus, cortex, cerebellum. Something reassuring, I felt, about all those brain parts. We're not just a gray soup up there. Then he said 'dementia,' and an abyss opened before us. Just said the word as if it were 'backache' or 'head cold,' and it went home. I knew by the way Grisha squeezed my hand. 'Tell me the name of my problem,' he'll say sometimes. 'Dysnomia,' I prefer to answer. An inoffensive word, and I'm hoping he'll remember it rather than the other one. Before long, he'll remember neither."

"You don't think he could have stepped out?" Gabriel swung open the kitchen door to see. Grisha was in his chair, head down. "You know, I've never seen him asleep before. He's so quiet. My father snored. Sawed down whole forests."

"One of my blessings is a husband who does not snore. May cut a bit of kindling now and then. But whole forests, no."

She blew her nose; with abandon she blew. "I believe that most men snore. But if you roll them onto their sides they usually leave off, for a while at least. That nice young neurologist — I believe he's a bachelor like you. Something told me so. I think you should meet him. Perhaps he does not snore." "Bachelor" was how she put it, not caring for the more modern terms. ("And where does he go to meet these young men?" she'd asked Marghie after chancing to run into Gabriel and an unpresentable character at the corner of Fifty-sixth and Kimbark. "Any bar or bunkhouse, Mom.")

"Should we wake him?" Gabriel asked.

"Yes, it's getting late. He's been hard to handle at bedtime." She rose. "More than once he's slept beside me in his clothes. And shoes. I sometimes have to force him to bathe."

When they went in and woke him, Grisha looked beseechingly around the room. He babbled something in Hungarian that alarmed Lilo and made her set her jaw. "Time for bed." More Hungarian. "Enough of that." More Hungarian. "Grisha!"

Halfway up the stairs, on Lilo's arm, he turned lucidly to Gabriel and said, "We have lost him."

"We'll find him," Gabriel answered.

"Not this time," Grisha said. "We have lost him," and went with Lilo to their room. Danny had lately pulled the old disappearing act, his signature from childhood. It was one thing for him to do that when he was talking. But now . . .

Although his eyes were heavy, Gabriel wanted to stay up a while longer. He tried out Grisha's chair, still warm. He noticed on the mantel some objects not there in previous summers, lares and penates from Fiftieth Street. He jumped up for a closer look at an old photograph, taken during or just after the war, it seemed. Lilo and Grisha were standing beside what Gabriel recognized as the lagoon in Lincoln Park, young marrieds smiling with all their teeth into the afternoon sun. A day in paradise, it appeared, till you noticed that she held a rose upside down. Signal of distress? Also given pride of place on the mantel was a photo taken on the porch of the lodge at Los Alamos with Oppie, their household divinity, frowning between them.

Since Danny's radical disappearance two months ago, it had seemed to Gabriel that what was occurring was a realization of sorts, for which Danny's senior thesis at Swarthmore could now be understood as the prospectus. It had been uncertain whether he'd get such a bizarre topic approved for honors work, but a malleable professor of American Studies consented. The subject? The vanished. Danny had worked with a will at it, his lair piled high with filthy clothes and books entitled *Judge Crater: Where Are You?, They Sailed into Oblivion, I Searched for Amelia, They Never Came Back, Boy and Girl Tramps of America, The Missingest Man in Milwaukee, No Earthly Explanation, Last Seen in Orange Socks, What Happened to Dorothy Arnold?* and *You Too Can Escape!*

Of particular interest to him was Sister Aimee Semple McPherson, who took up a whole chapter. In receipt of the "clarion call that brooks no denial," hollering out her heart for Christ, Sister made a hit. On the day of her disappearance, it was speculated that members of the southern California underworld had rubbed her out for saying in a sermon that she'd rather see her children in their graves than in a Venice dance hall. After the disappearance, her faithful raised a reward of twenty-five thousand for Aimee. An informant slunk forward to say that she was either in the mountains back of Santa Barbara or else on the banks of the Santa Ynez River. She turned up in Mexico, exhausted but alive and telling some story about being kidnapped and taken across the border. Cock-and-bull; she'd disappeared for love of a married man, her radio operator, which was strange, because she'd always said that the guy of her dreams would be tall, pious, and above all a trombone player. Kenneth G. Ormiston was none of these. Sister stood trial for having staged her disappearance to join him. Obstructing a criminal investigation and using the mails to defraud were alleged, charges she narrowly issued from.

Or how about another of Danny's favorites, Nila Cook? She was an American follower of Gandhi, but so wayward that the Mahatma actually went on a twenty-one-day fast to atone for how *native* she'd gone. Then, as suddenly as she'd turned up, Nila vanished from the ashram, declaring, "I don't care what people think! I want speed! I want flight! I want to attend orchestra dances!" Gandhi was heartsick about it.

Take the extraordinary case of Mrs. William B. Fellows of

Cambridge, Mass., of whom Danny gave a detailed account. After three years of marriage she took a powder. Not a word from Eulalie Fellows. Twenty years later Mr. Fellows came home to find her in the kitchen, cooking dinner. Refusing to divulge where she'd been, what she'd done, Eulalie submitted to the marital yoke for three more years before lighting out again, this time for good.

Take Lydie Marland of Ponca City, Oklahoma. She was the adopted daughter and wife — yes, both — of Ernest Whitworth Marland, oil baron and former governor. Lydie sashayed out of town one afternoon and was next located twelve years later in a motel outside of Independence, Missouri, dressed in a tacky squaw's outfit, making up beds to pay her rent, hiding in terror whenever a car with an Oklahoma license plate passed by.

Still more interesting, according to Danny, were the vanishing menfolk. Alfred Easton Vermeule, for instance, a bank president who disappeared from Grosse Point Farms, Michigan, to be discovered fifteen years later working as a circus clown in Pensacola. Or William Daniel of Brooklyn, who stepped out for a pack of cigarettes and was next identified twenty-nine years later in San Francisco. He *said* he'd lit out because a play he wrote hadn't made it to Broadway. Then there was Dr. Charles F. Hastings of Pittsburgh, who went up to Erie, changed his name to John Hugh, and opened a pet shop. "My real name was too fancy," he said. How about Thomas O'Grady, who relocated from Williamsburg, Virginia, to the Sandwich Islands and refused to come home even when twenty-two years later his mother caught up with him? How about James Sarsfield of Normal, Illinois, who arrived at the 1939 New York World's Fair, sent his best friend a souvenir cigar from the mailing office, and then went missing promptly and forever into the fifth dimension of Flushing Meadow? And how about a physician from Jersey City named Larry L. Fader? While scuba diving near the Statue of Liberty he disappeared. Two months later his wife got a letter from Amarillo saying, "I ran away to get out of the old dying rut. Yours very affly."

Scheherezade of the gone missing, Danny held you till sun-up with this vast accumulation. The so-called humanities weren't too bad after all, Gabriel concluded, if they could bear such lunatic fruit as *Here and Gone* — best honors thesis anybody ever wrote at Swarthmore, some said.

Now he went upstairs, undressed, got in bed. Danny's bedstead, bureau, slicker in the closet, old wristwatch on the nightstand, down-at-heel Wallabees under the bed. Sweet smell of Dan in the pitch pine of the floor and walls. He drifted off, then bolted upright. A roughhouse was being raised out on the lake. Loons. First one, then another, then a chorus. They cut loose with the love cry. Then with the happiness. Then the danger, the panic. Gabriel put Danny's pillow over his head, hummed a tune so as not to hear.

— four —

1977: SANCTUARY

He'd expected, on arrival there three years earlier, not even to notice Chicago. Instead he couldn't get enough. Of the skyline for starters — a work of art, particularly if you walked out to Adler Planetarium and turned around quick for a look. This Sunday morning Chicago wavered in the heat. He went in for the air-conditioning, then decided to stick around, and took a seat in the next-to-last row. One of life's loveliest occasions, after all, is to rest in the cool of a planetarium, waiting for the show to start. Nothing very bad could happen to you here. The pinks and oranges of sunset lit the dome. A sickle moon stood midway up the eastern sky. Venus brightened, followed by the host of stars. The western rays settled out. The refrigerated twilight carried him back to summer afternoons at the St. Charles Parish Planetarium, a lesser star show no doubt but with pride of place for Gabriel over every other.

The projector rose from the floor, looking like a pterodactyl pierced all over, pouring light. Children yelped with pleasure. Now Orion showed forth boldface in the eastern sky, all the dots connected. Now Perseus, Taurus, Gemini, Canis Major. Gabriel was enjoying himself as if all of it were news to him. Against the backdrop of the Milky Way, Cassiopeia was featured with a bit of commentary — not altogether accurate but so what? Then a meteor shower drenched the crowd. A weird covered honking voice behind him said, "Bootiful!" and groaned. Gabriel knew that voice. But from where? From three Fridays ago when Marghie had run *The Hunchback of Notre Dame.* "This is a picture about what it means to be a living gargoyle, to have a sloppy drooling grin and a gigantic eyeball and a hump on your back the size of Annapurna. Forget that lousy extra thumb of yours!" The hunchback taking the Gypsy girl Esmeralda (ah, those inescapable Gypsies) to the heights of the cathedral and crying out from his perch, "Sanctooary! Sanctooary!" — this was the big leagues of pathos. Gabriel turned to see by starlight that seated behind him was no Quasimodo. A matinee idol was more like it. A diminutive Latin lover was more like it. Smiles were exchanged. The Cook's tour of the galaxy faded out as, in the full spate of curiosity, these two contrived to get nearer. The little fellow hit the deck and reappeared by Gabriel's side. He was seriously small to have done that. Now he rubbed his hands together, as if for a task, took Gabriel by the hand, and settled back to watch the show, as simply as that. Gabriel felt an exploratory pressure applied to his double thumb. Very slowly, very smilingly, under cover of the night sky and by a mutual certitude, their lips connected.

He was, Gabriel was to learn, Heberto Huesca, deaf as a post. Later that afternoon, the two of them seated at the lip of Buckingham Fountain, he taught Gabriel to sign the letters of the alphabet, then a few basic words, including "beautiful," "wonderful," "happy," "gay," "deaf," "hearing," "love," "sex," and "silly." "Silly" was a *y* waved vigorously across the forehead. "Sex" was the base of one palm banged against the other. "Love" was a self-embrace. "Hearing" was a circle described in front of the mouth. "Deaf" was a finger touching the ear, then the lips. "Gay" was a *g* applied to the chin. "Happy" was an open hand moving up and off the chest. "Wonderful" was the palms pumping skyward. "Beautiful" was the fingers opening to circle the face, then regrouping at the chin. Heberto began showing him the same words in Spanish sign, but Gabriel begged him to stop. One language at a time, he spelled out defectively on his fingers.

Fishing around for something easy to say, Gabriel pointed to himself and signed two *g*'s, then pointed to Heberto and signed two *h*'s. For he had a theory about people graced with double initials. He'd made a mental list and there wasn't a dud in the bunch. Noble destinies awaited everybody with double initials and he wanted to tell Heberto, but spelling this out one letter at a time was too arduous, so he settled for, *T-w-o i-n-i-t-i-a-l-s, g-o-o-d l-u-c-k*. Berto looked perplexed but smiled politely. "Berto," was what to call him. It suited.

A mist from the fountain had got them pleasantly wet. Heading now down Michigan Avenue, they dried off in the warmth of the afternoon, spelling with their hands, working up a semi-private sign. Berto was alternately amused and offended by Gabriel's improvisations. As when, among Hottentots, you mean "We want to toast your health" but say "We mean to roast your child," he was signing things he did not intend. There was plenty of room for individual expressiveness in the realm of American Sign Language, but there were rules too and these had to be mastered. Gabriel was properly chastened. "How about a little dinner?" he signed, to perfection. A vigorous nod of the fist, meaning yes. On the way to the Emperor's Choice, Berto taught him another score of signs.

"I - eat - anything," he assured Gabriel. They had hot and sour soup and tangy spicy kidney and dried string beans and lychees. And when the fortune cookies were set before them Berto ate one of those too, fortune and all, before Gabriel could stop him.

Over the course of the next few weeks his little apartment filled up, one belonging at a time, with the evidence of Berto, till two thirds of the clothes in the drawers and the closet were no longer his. He came home one evening to find that a hook had been bolted into the ceiling and Berto's ten-speed hung from it. A collection of little giraffes — Berto's totemic animal, evidently — congregated in the windowsills. He bathed, never showered, and the shelves over the toilet were increasingly crowded with an armada of the little boats Berto liked to launch on his bathwater.

Linus Pauling had come to speak that autumn in Mandel Hall, and during the Q and A an undergraduate asked the great chemist if out of the vastness of his experience of nature and of humankind there was one final wisdom, one culminating piece of advice he could impart. "Find somebody you can get along with," Pauling said, "and settle down." Marghie had shown Gabriel his share of screwball comedies over the years and they all ended the same, with two people, after lengthy and purblind struggle, *settling down*. There seemed to be a large-scale prejudice in favor of this solution to life's dilemmas. Having despaired of it, he awakened one morning to discover himself among the coupled. So be it, he declared, if such is the accord that's found me.

11:30 P.M.: If boyfriends were an item ordered from a catalog, would I have chosen a deaf one? No. But whom would I have chosen? Somebody forbearing, kind, sweet-smelling, smart. B is all these. Have reached the point where I can sign what I like. Still, the communication is all primary colors, as if we were applying the emotional equipment of childhood to adult work. A lot of the time I feel lonely when I'm with him. I keep talking to my Imaginary Friend even though there's a real one on hand. (About I.F.: I realize after a lifetime of larking around with him that he's my TWIN, my IDENTICAL twin, with all due respect to Marghie and Danny. I don't think he looks much like me though. Much handsomer.) Think B feels lonely too. Goes out a lot and a couple of times has come home very late. Out tonight again. Why am I not jealous? On account of my Imaginary Friend, with me always though he's metamorphosed over the years? Has gotten worldlier and more skeptical. Has gotten less hopeful. Takes a dim view of my new home life. May be hatching a plot to oust Berto. Can smile and smile and be a villain.

In New Orleans last weekend. First time in almost a year. Mom says what makes her serene is to know I'm flourishing. If I had a child I'd never be serene again. I'd be harrowed with worry. Come to think of it, "worried to death" was one of Mom's favorite phrases. I'd be a literal case of that if I were a parent. Having B around is bad enough.

She never put herself first till Dad was dead and I was in the clear. And it cost her. All that getting sick. I think it's turned me against illness. If somebody's under the weather, I change the subject. If somebody calls to say somebody's in the hospital, I hang up. Better work on this. Be counter-phobic. Do what you fear, as great sages say.

I think it must have been Mom's credo too. She did what she feared. (Married him.) Now she does what she wants. After he died, she said a great silence had come into the house. Late one night last summer when I visited, something strange went on. It was late, I was upstairs. She was down in the kitchen, padding around. I heard her speaking in a low register. It was clear from the content what she was doing — speaking in Dad's voice. Doing a pretty fair imitation too. Instead of hearing him all the time, as when he was alive, she evidently hears him now only when she feels like it. Oh, the same bloviations, same displeasures. Same determination to silence the rest of us. Fundamentally, Milt could not stand the sound of anybody else's voice. Opinions other than his own? He spat on them. Referred to those he disagreed with as mental cases. But nowadays Dad offers his views when and only when Mom permits. By God, she survived him (and survived the unholy combination of him and me.)

2:45 A.M.: *Milt and I are getting along better. Now he's dead the great conversation begins, Geismar to Geismar.*

4:50 A.M.: *Still waiting for Berto.*

6:00 A.M.: *Marg says there's a psychoanalyst who talks about "good-enough mothers." Mom's been good enough and then some. Is one really good parent as much as you can hope for? Is it greedy to expect two? But the makeweight to thoughts like these is what filled my mind in the weeks after Dad died — how he came home one afternoon, happy as I ever saw him, saying "I got it!" And what "it" turned out to be was a Braille watch he wanted to give as a present to Lou and Madelyn Feldman's son. Now that I think about it, he did lots of favors for people. Lou and Madelyn were reputed to be the poorest Jews in town. They had a son, very prematurely born, who'd lost his eyesight in a faulty incubator. You'd think at least a generous settlement would have come out of that, but no, their advertise-in-the-newspaper-type lawyer failed to make the case. Dad said God had given the Feldmans their own troubles to suffer, plus other people's too. "And you bellyache about every little thing." (He was right. I did have a tendency to bellyache.) People pitied but also feared the Feldmans on account of their extraordinary bad luck. When the son, the blind one, Eliot — called Buddy — had his bar mitzvah, many of the best-off congregants chipped in generously for the oneg shabbat. And when Buddy Feldman chanted his Torah portion, reading it out of a Braille Pentateuch, there was open crying among the grown-ups, and unendurable embarrassment among their children.*

In the days and weeks after Dad died, what I kept remembering was that Braille watch, and how he drove over to the Feldmans' to give it to Buddy.

Sunrise: Berto not coming home, I guess. Could I just as well have ended up with a blind boyfriend? Doubt it. Buddy Feldman always scared me.

Berto did come home — that afternoon, without much in the way of an explanation; excitedly showed Gabriel something he'd found in the park, a pinkish-white chrysalis, and put it in the dresser among their socks and shorts and T-shirts. It was dark and warm in there, and some days later, when Gabriel opened the drawer, out flew an immense moth, powdery green and with fantastical antennae, who hung still as death on the curtains, then made for the open window. Two sets of eyes adorned the wings when the moth flared them. Gabriel had read his Fabre, but you couldn't know about that particular moth from Fabre. No, that had been the famed luna moth, a strictly New World creature. Before bed that night, he got up enough courage to show the empty chrysalis to Berto.

"Here - and - gone. - Flew- right - out - the - window."

"I'll - punch - your - head," Berto signed back, fit to be tied. "You - should - have - stopped - him."

"Oh - go - to - sleep."

"He - was - *mine*." The hands flew smartly.

"Go - to - sleep."

"Describe - first."

"He - stared - at - me - with - his - wings. - Mint - green - and - they - had - a - sort - of - dark - brown - edge - to - them. - White - body." All of this as best Gabriel could manage in sign.

"Big?"

"Enormous. - Go - to - sleep."

Berto sighed and off he went, unaware that the force of gravity decreases by the inverse of the square of the distance. And do I love him, Gabriel wondered, for the mighty reaches of his ignorance? On a weekend trip to the Indiana Dunes, Gabriel had pointed out a vaguely reddish star at one corner of Orion and explained that this was Betelgeuse, a red giant, swelling up gigantically because the supply of hydrogen at its core is all out. When our own sun does this, in about three billion years, the oceans will boil. "You - make - these - things - up - to - scare - people," said Berto. Gabriel had observed in him a programmatic skepticism, as childlike in its way as total credulity would have been. Then is it simply that I want a child by my side? But he didn't like this train of thought and always stopped it cold.

It is so easy, he reflected, alone now at his desk, to imagine other, stillborn universes in which nothing diversifies because nothing survives. Among the improbable wonders of this one is that at length, and without trying, it produced an organism that asks questions — some of them unanswerable because meaningless but others, the so-called scientific ones, very much to the point. Our presence was designless happenstance, the outcome of contingencies, of course. All teleological thinking was anathema to him. There must be no "and yet" here, no smuggling in of any anthropic principle. The cosmos did not know we were coming. We happened along as fortuitously as everything else. And yet . . . *Stop it.* And yet . . . *Stop.* And yet there are sufficient stars in just the Milky Way that if just one in a hundred of them is orbited by a planet like our own, that already amounts to more than a billion Earth-like places in the galaxy. And when you consider the tens of billions of other galaxies — spiral, elliptical, irregular — and the thousands of billions of planets plausibly within them, it seems a little perverse to go on claiming we're the one-time-only accident. If not as fundamentally a part of the show as gravity or electromagnetism, neither are we just a fluke. Granted, we were not here at the daybreak of the universe, nor will be for its long, perhaps eternally long, twilight. The cosmos did not know *Homo sapiens sapiens* was coming, was neither glad of our arrival, nor will be grieved when we go. But we will have been here . . . And presto, there it was again, anthropism, that old bugbear, rearing its self-important head.

His doctorate was to be awarded a year ahead of schedule. In several sieges of calculation, he'd put together a self-consistent account, acceptable to his teachers, of what the universe, a mere fourteen billion years in age, will be like one hundred trillion years from now — on the assumption that the amount of dark matter is insufficient to cause it, at some future time, to begin to contract and that, accordingly, expansion will continue indefinitely. Big assumption, and upon it all his reckonings were based. The idea of a universe grown ineffably old beckoned to Gabriel. In about a trillion years, as he figured it, the formation of new stars will be a thing of the past. The lowest mass should be out of fuel about a hundred trillion years after that. What will be left? Relics, dodderers: white dwarfs, brown dwarfs, neutron stars. And black holes, of course.

The phone rang. "Hello?"

"You sitting down?" It was Marghie, who'd scared him before with that line. "I've got news." Danny could be dead; she'd announce it without tears, like this. She'd call and say, "You sitting down?" and detail the grisly circumstances: that he'd floated ashore along the Upper Peninsula, that his head and hands had been found in a garbage can in Bolivia, that he was a smear at the bottom of Copper Canyon. *"We went and got married!"* she crowed. So Peter Storrow had prevailed. That prig, married to her.

Gabriel cleared his throat grimly. "Tell me once, and I won't ask again. Why did you marry him?"

"Because he's no odder than the love choices of some I could mention. And he's loopy about me. And we're going to have babies galore. And we can't wait."

"You're —"

"Not yet. Trying for all we're worth though." Gabriel had stopped listening. For suddenly there was bigger news by far, news worthy of waking Berto for. Marghie nattered on about her domestic plans while he beheld the prodigal come home, the luna, perched at the windowsill, opening and closing his stark-staring wings, who made now for a shelf, crawled in behind a row of books. "And we're going to Quebec City for a honeymoon . . . " Did she understand that she was making him thoroughly sick? Oh, she understood.

"I'm *happy* for you, Marg."

"Doesn't sound that way. Sounds like maybe you're too busy with your little jumping bean to care."

"Let's talk when you're back from Quebec. Congrats to the lucky guy." A silence. "Marg, any word? I know, nothing. Just need to ask."

"He's around. We've had more letters, if you want to call them that. Just a bunch of newspaper and magazine clippings, really. I think the postmarks are misleading. I think he sends them to weird places and has people mail the letters for him."

"Why would he do that?"

"Because he's still got his sense of fun."

"Does he realize the pain he's causing? It's well over a year now."

"Nearly two. He must be finding work of some kind. I like to think he's okay. Maybe even talking again. Kicking butt and taking names. Hang on, hang on." Hand over receiver, muffled exchange. "Peter says hi. Say hi, Peter." Peter's solemn baritone came through.

"Tell Peter I'm seeing the Dunallens next week in New York. I'm going there for a conference at Rockefeller. We're going, I mean."

"You and —"

"Berto, yes."

"Gabe and Berto and Ellie and Ned? A double date?"

"Yep."

"Extraordinary. Did you mention to them that he's Mario Lanza?"

"I said I'm coming to New York with a friend. She said, 'Bring him, by all means.' Said, 'We'll take in a concert and have supper.' I said, 'Ellie, my friend is deaf.' She didn't miss a beat, she said, 'We'll go to the *ballet* and have supper.' I thought that was class."

"Of *course* you did. Ellie and Ned Dunallen are not the object of a fan club. No, it's much more like a religion. There are people, and you'll be one, who when you say 'Dunallen' will get so dewy-eyed you'd think Bambi had minced into the room."

"You really don't like them."

'I *do* like them. It's simply that they need saving from their admirers, as I have explained to my *bridegroom* here. Nearly had to break his little arm. If you go getting sticky and sloppy about Ned and Ellie Dunallen, I'll break yours. Ballet and supper, indeed!" She hung up.

But to ballet and supper they went, two weeks later. Ned had instructed them to drop by for a drink beforehand. The Dunallens' apartment building, a cavernous sandstone pile, overlooked Gramercy Park. A birdcage elevator, manned by a specter in uniform, took Gabriel and Berto to the second floor. A housemaid let them into the apartment and showed them to the living room, where Ellie and Ned rose to greet them. It occurred to Gabriel that he was seeing these two for the first time in their city clothes. She had on a close-fitting brown woolen dress and a double strand of pearls, and looked any woman's dream of sixty. He wore a black suit and an askew bowtie and looked nearer, my God, to thee. Gabriel hugged the skin and bones beneath the clothes, kissed Elise, then preformed the necessary introductions, inclining this way and that, signing and spelling. Berto spontaneously gave Ellie a kiss, to everybody's pleasure. They were off to a roaring start.

Every vertical surface was book-lined. Much of the library appeared old — complete sets of Carlyle, Thackeray, Dickens, Ruskin, Macaulay. An upright plainness was, at this address, the rule. Carpets were down to the warp and weft. Drapes were faded. Furniture was the lovingly handed-on kind. Above window seats the leaded panes gave onto bare treetops. "Come warm yourselves," said Elise. "Ned's laid a fire."

Gabriel noted over the mantelpiece an engraving identical to one he'd seen in their dining room at Portage. It showed, according to the gloss underneath, the gods Jupiter and Mercury saying to

Baucis and Philemon, whoever they were, "You, just man, and you, his worthy wife — declare what thing you most desire!"

"You know, I saw this at your place last summer."

Elise said, "The two engravings were in my maternal grandmother's family. She and her brother, my great Uncle Ogden, had married in the same year. Each couple received one. Somehow Uncle Ogden's and Granny's both made their way to my own parents' attic. Let's sit in front of the fire, it's so lovely. Once when we were in Seattle, Ned and I dusted them off and asked if we might have them. One went to Wisconsin, the other came here. Ned can tell you better than I what the myth is."

He returned from the sideboard with glasses and a bottle of wine. He poured, then raised a glass, said, "Happy days!" Superb toast, Gabriel thought, implying the fragility of all this order. Now Ned turned his attention to the engraving. "Jupiter and Mercury have disguised themselves as wayfarers, and when they pass through Phrygia and ask for shelter, every door slams shut against them. But at the hut of old Philemon and Baucis they are invited in."

"I've heard this story. It's Lot and his wife," Gabriel said.

"Weirdly similar, I know. But different. Baucis sets out olives and curdled cheese and roasted eggs and radishes —"

"This," said Elise, "is why Ned has to tell it. He gets in all the good details."

"— and a bowl of wine. Then she serves a meal of cabbage and smoked ham. This old couple are poor, remember. Their table's no good, it wobbles, so Baucis sticks a broken piece of pottery under one leg. For dessert she puts out plums and dates and figs and nuts and red grapes and apples and a honeycomb." This was tough sledding to put into sign. Gabriel radically simplified the bill of fare. "And then Philemon and Baucis realize that a miracle is taking place. The wine bowl keeps brimming up, no matter how much they pour out. Philemon and Baucis know now that these wayfarers are not what they seem. 'Follow us up the mountain path,' Jupiter and Mercury say."

"Slower, honey," said Elise. "The boy's breaking a sweat from all this interpreting." It was true. While Berto, for his part, sat there thoroughly mystified.

"So up the path they go, and they turn round to see all of Phrygia devoured by mud."

"By a swamp, actually," said Elise. *S-w-a-m-p*, Gabriel spelled.

"Yes, all except for the house of Baucis and Philemon, which has turned into a temple. The gods command them to go and tend it for the rest of their days. Then they ask what they're asking there in the engraving — 'What do you two want most?' He glanced at both guests to be sure they were up to speed (which Berto wasn't.) "Ellie likes to tell the rest."

Had they learned this portioning out of a good story from Lilo and Grisha? Possibly Lilo and Grisha had learned it from them. It was in any case the token of true marriage, Gabriel thought. "To die together is what they want most," Elise said. "And the gods consent. Years later, at the destined hour, Baucis looks up at her Philemon and sees that he's turning into an oak. And Philemon sees that his Baucis is becoming a linden. They have just enough time to say goodbye before the bark seals up their mouths. And side by side, somewhere in Phrygia, that oak and that linden are standing to this day, grown together at the crowns." Clearly, these two had been bedtime storytellers of a very high order. And with children, or the equivalent of children, in the house again, they couldn't resist, even though it wasn't bedtime.

It was ballet time, so up from Gramercy Park they hastened in a Checker, Gabriel and Berto riding the jump seats. A makeshift family, of one night's duration, had declared itself. "You are going," Ned told the boys, "to see the work of the greatest choreographer who ever lived." He reported this not as opinion but knowledge.

G-r-e-a-t-e-s-t c-h-o-r-e-o-g-r-a-p-h-e-r. "I had no understanding of ballet till Ellie schooled me to it. Seemed like so much jumping around. I thought it a desecration of the music, till gradually I began to see what she was seeing."

They crossed town at Fifty-ninth and headed up Broadway. Lincoln Center came into view on the left. Gabriel's watch said three minutes to eight. Calling it close. "We've seven minutes' grace," Elise assured him. Ned paid the driver. Across the plaza and through the theater lobby they hurried and up to their seats in the second row of the first ring, as the house lights dimmed and applause broke out for the spotlit conductor. Now the curtain, turning in the glow of the footlights from gold to orange, rose on what Ned's untutored eyes had originally seen, a bunch of posing preening smiling acrobats. It was a tedium to watch; Gabriel closed his eyes and listened to the music. Intermittent applause erupted throughout, then a mad ovation at the curtain call.

What did people see in this? Gabriel knew that New York in recent years had gone ballet-crazy. Crazy was the only word to describe some of the conversations overheard at intermission among the adepts:

"I understand Helgi has bruised his coccyx."

"Merrill is at the top of her bent tonight. That quadruple pirouette in the adagio!"

Several spoke of having witnessed a ballerina of the despised competing troupe fall on stage the previous evening — Gelsey had cracked up. You'd think they'd seen the *Titanic* go down.

"Suzanne has taken to doing sixes instead of quatres in the entrechat."

"We are in awe of Colleen's soutenu turns!"

Though Ned and Elise smiled indulgently at this acumen, their devotion was aloof from all commentary. They chose silence in face of the Eleusinian mysteries, and steered their guests to the bar.

"You - are - a - good - sport," Gabriel signed quickly to Berto. Bottoms up and a bell rang, urging the audience back to their seats.

The curtain rose on a boy and girl standing side by side. He extended a hand to her. Like thunder it broke on Gabriel as, out of this one gesture, the variety of love and separateness was elaborated: the interdepending, the standing alone — the instability. No story here, and because there was no story the movements could be about everything. The dance he saw for what it was, a clear morning world in which each emotion stood forth, divinized; he got it, got what the shouting was about. And, indeed, at the conclusion unrestrained shouting did pour from the upper rings, and confetti, and nobody would let up till the Master himself, white-faced and beaming and with a scarlet kerchief at his throat, peeped out twice from the curtain to wave goodnight.

Berto was not just a good sport; he'd got a kick out of all this high aesthetical pandemonium. "Good - as - extra - innings - at - Comiskey," he signed, and Gabriel translated. The heads of the grown-ups went back in unison.

At a nearby restaurant — Gabriel's precise notion of what a New York restaurant should be: a sideboard spread with phantasmagorical desserts, murals throughout of cavorting nudies and men in leopard hides — the staff greeted the Dunallens as dignitaries. The maître d' bent to Elise's hand, though without the presumption of actual contact, then wrung Ned's with the same Hapsburgian correctness, neither overly familiar nor lacking in warmth, three firm shakes, and showed the foursome to their table. With drinks before them, Ned sighed, smiled, said, "How generous the arrangements are." Gabriel translated, then added in sotto-voce sign, "I - think - he - means - being - with - us." Elise recommended the chicken paprikash or the sturgeon schnitzel. And there was a beautiful carrot soup to start with. Or the tomato herring.

She and Ned were on their way to Mexico later that week, and in high spirits about the trip. Amateur pteridologists, they traveled annually with the American Fern Society to Oaxaca. Gabriel had known his share of bird-watchers, and if anybody on earth was purer of heart than that bunch, it must be this one, the fern-watchers. Elise and Ned were serious amateurs. They'd been to the rain forests of Costa Rica and Hawaii. They'd been to the Rockies, the Adirondacks. They'd been eight times to Oaxaca. Elise was credited in the literature with having discovered, near Hierve el Agua, a new species of selaginella. "You'd be surprised," Ned said, "how often it's nonprofessionals who make these finds."

"Well, you know, it's sometimes ham astronomers who first observe comets. Supernovae too. I think I'd like to have lived back when all of science was amateurs. Newton, Dalton, Mendel, Darwin, Mendeleyev. What else were they?" Here came their appetizers. "I'm curious about Mexico. Raised so close by, but I've never been there. Berto's Mexican, but he's never been there either."

"Oh, we first began going a long time ago, before we even had the girls. Ellie discovered her fern in forty-nine."

"I was *very* young, you understand."

"You won't believe it, but in those days people used to mistake us for brother and sister," said Ned. "It no longer happens, of course. Ellie's still a young woman. I am as you see me."

"Salt and pepper, please," said Berto intelligibly.

"Tell us what's ahead for you — for you both, I mean," said Elise.

"Um, Berto is a little unsure about what he wants to do. I get my doctorate next month, and I'm in the running for an assistant professorship in my department. I think I may get it."

"If I were a betting man," said Ned, "and come to think of it I am, I'd lay odds that you will, Gabriel."

"You, a betting man? I wouldn't have guessed."

"One day when I was about seven, and the century was about fifteen, I went with my father to the races in Terre Haute. I got a sudden hunch on a horse called Drummer. Father bet three dollars, on my behalf. I went hot and cold and broke a fever. Drummer paid eight to one. By the time we got home, I had whooping cough. And there's the whole of my betting career."

Gabriel was bushed in his hands. A lot of Elise and Ned's talk came across, if at all, in pidgin sign, making Berto furrow his brow. But he'd got the drill: these very grown-up people from the fancy upper reaches took turns telling stories about the things that had happened to them. Easy enough to play. Berto leapt in with an inconsequent narrative of his own, speaking not signing it. He told about how bad seventh grade had been. His voice shifted to falsetto with emotion. That year, he said, he'd been forced to ride the retard bus. Gabriel repeated the phrases to make them comprehensible. Even the immense social skills of the Dunallens might prove unequal to this. Their faces were masks; they were stumped for what to say. But then Elise reached out for Berto's head of gleaming black hair and tucked a lock behind an ear, and said something about how fine it was say goodbye to the indignities of childhood. Gabriel signed it.

"The poet Shelley," said Ned, "wore a ring on his finger engraved with 'the good time will come.' It's what I used to repeat to myself the whole way home from school, on the moral imbecile bus, which I was forced to ride." And, against the odds, Gabriel signed it, very pleased with his growing fluency.

Did a vile word ever pass between Ellie and Ned, these paragons? Must have. But the strongly idealizing bent of their marriage seemed to have woven the fury into the silk. You idealize me, I'll idealize you, and we'll become ideal. Being with them was like hearing a song. You couldn't be sure of what you were hearing till the song was done. And when would that be? "The time for making up your mind about people is — *never*!" Marghie liked to say, quoting Hepburn, as so often, from *Philadelphia Story*. About the Dunallens, anyhow, Gabriel saw no reason to make up his mind. Grant the mysterious their mystery, they have earned it.

After dinner, as they pulled on their coats, Elise turned to survey the room. "We used to come here with Grisha and Lilo whenever they visited. In those days it was a stifling, gloomy, boiled-beef kind of place. Grisha loved it. Lilo accepted it."

"Then," said Ned, "we brought them back after the new management came in, and Lilo was enchanted, and Grisha considered the air-conditioning and the excellent food a profanation of our old times." He changed register. "My last few letters to them have gone unanswered. For more than two months now. In her last, Lilo said Daniel had been traveling, and that Grisha had a very bad cold." And hearing this, Gabriel knew that he was alone inside the Hundert circle, that the depths were shared only with him. "Anyhow, we'll have night after night with them this summer," Ned continued. "She was very firm about renewing the lease in Portage, thank heavens. Some things are too sacred to change. Or am I daring the gods when I talk like that?"

"You are daring the gods," said Elise as she entered the revolving door. "A thing I've warned you about." Out at the curb, she said goodbye to Berto with both hands and a kiss, then the same to Gabriel, along with a look that was between them. "He's lovely," she said in his ear, not bothering to whisper. Firmly, Ned kissed both young men, stepped back. "I am," he said, "too old to blush."

———

They came home to the luna, plying its wings at the edge of a bowl of sugar water they'd set out before leaving. The weeks went by. Berto got quieter. (He *said* less; the kitchen commotions of metal on metal were as fierce as ever. Gabriel hadn't known how loud the deaf are.) One evening Berto went in search of the moth, unseen for two days, and found him clinging to a dust-kitten under the bed. He peered in with a flashlight and cried, very intelligibly, "He's had babies!" Indeed, there was a mass of eggs. Berto scooped them into a coffee cup and hoped for the best.

Gray and early one morning of the following week, the phone rang. An amused, leisurely voice said to Gabriel, "Your morals aren't all they ought to be. And everybody knows it." The delivery was ostentatiously southern, one of those all-purpose drawls corresponding to nowhere in particular.

"Who is this?"

A hiss from between what sounded like clenched teeth. *"Narcissist!"* This word, produced with sudden savagery, had lately come into vogue. *"Poseur!"* That one less so. Under cover of anonymity, some venomous somebody was choosing his aspersions with care. *"DIRTY COCKSUCKER!"* Gabriel checked an impulse to hang up. He wanted to hear what was coming next. He heard plenty: "You may have fooled a few old fools, *but the rest of us are onto you.* I happen to know there are *faked* data in your so-called dissertation. Faked *calculations*, too. *Forty-five* faked calculations. You faked the whole goddamned thing, didn't you? TOO BUSY SUCKING MEXICAN DICK, FROM WHAT I HEAR!" The caller was uncertain on some consonants; the caller, at seven fifteen A.M., was stewed to the gills. He'd begun to cry, it sounded like. "I hope you get syph and clap both you, you *queen*, you . . ." But he'd run out of epithets, and took a new tack. "I hear you're not like most of these fags. They go for big dicks. You like little ones. Little Mexican dicks —"

It was getting time to hang up. The fact, however, was just as this abusive mongrel said: Like the Greeks of old, Gabriel admired small penises. That much was truth. The alleged forty-five faked calculations were another matter. Nothing in those pages was faked.

But the southern accent with which his tormentor was speaking was. And what Gabriel heard seeping up from underneath the phony twang was the guy's real accent, the unloveliest accent of all. "Forty-five" came out as "farty-five." So it was that fellow from St. Louis who'd been drummed out of the graduate program the previous spring. What the hell was his name? Ross Something or Something Ross. Gabriel slammed down the receiver hard enough, he hoped, to break the eardrum at the other end. That evening he put a whistle beside the phone, to have handy. He'd literally blow the whistle on Something Ross if he ever called again. He'd knock the bastard's head off. Had enough on his mind this morning without marauders ringing up. Berto hadn't come home. Again.

Love was the collision of two fantasies, he'd decided — two fantasies, each dark to the other. Fine. The mutual darkness he could accept since love, though founded in fantasy, was the realest of real things, living sanctuary of mutual attention, daily witnessing of another, escape from selfishness, best of best, realest and best. Be my safehold, I will be yours. Then, on one side, the consent to be witnessed breaks. For the happiness you've known, you must pay full lick. That weekend, Berto rotated a fist across his heart, sign for sorry, packed up his giraffes and boats, his moth and her unhatched, dried-up eggs, his ten-speed, and was gone, the hook in the ceiling being all that remained of him.

five

IN THE GREAT WORLD

Portage, summer, 1979; Marghie home again, divorced these past two years. Not since Ethel Merman married Ernest Borgnine had there been such a mismatch as hers with Peter Storrow. "Don't speak that rotter's name!" she said to everybody, quoting. Or, "Go on and laugh. I'm laughing myself." Divorce became her. When Gabriel woke up, there she was at the foot of his bed. It was barely day — a fine one, filtering in through the curtains.

"I did it."

"What?"

"Broke open his strongbox —" Danny had mailed it to her the previous week, a gunmetal gray container with DO NOT OPEN, EVER. (THIS MEANS YOU, MARG!) painted across the top in what looked like fingernail polish.

"Marg —"

"With a screwdriver. It wasn't so hard." Gabriel sat up in bed and saw that she had it there in her lap, wide open. "A lot of things," she said, rooting around. "Some newspaper clippings about him. A picture of the two of us at the Indiana Dunes. A picture of Mom. A Polaroid of you, naked as a jaybird. Tummy sucked in, chest thrown out. Looks like you're pretending to be a muscle man. Looks like it was taken in the woods somewhere." She handed the Polaroid to him.

"At the Crum. One day we decided to go down there and take each other's picture. Don't see why you have to go snooping through his things, Marg. Thought we'd agreed not to."

"This isn't Tut's tomb, you know. No curse attaches to busting into it. Sooner or later everything gets rifled. Look what else is here." She took from the box a well-worn map of Southeast Asia, unfolded it, spread it on the bed. "I do like maps," she said. "The world looks so benign on them. Just pastel-colored places."

Also in the strongbox was a book in French — not a language Danny could read — entitled *Cambodge: année zéro*. The pages were uncut. And a crumbling two-volume work called *Central Parts of Indo-China: Cambodia and Laos*. The title page said 1864. She showed Gabriel the University of Chicago Library plate in the flyleaf of volume one. Dan had stolen this rarity, or else, to think better of him, owed six years of fines. Many of the pages were dog-eared. "Let me have a look at that," said Gabriel. Writing in library books had been a long suit of Danny's; he wanted to see what was inked into these two. The title page of volume one Dan had illuminated with questions and declarations: *What is the price of experience? do men buy it for a song? Or wisdom for a dance in the street? No, it is bought with the price Of all that a man hath: his house, his wife, his children.* The author of the two-volume work, one Henri Mouhot, had died of malaria at the Laotian border, said the preface, while writing up his travels. When carried off "in the flower of youth" he had been trying to discover a southern route into China by following the Mekong north. His manuscript, preserved by Cambodian bearers, was eventually returned to the dead man's family. " 'On the 27th April, 1858," Gabriel read from chapter one, "I embarked at London, in a sailing ship of very modest pretensions, in order to put in execution my long-cherished project of exploring the kingdoms of Siam, Cambodia, and Laos, and visiting the tribes who occupy the banks of the great river Mekon. I spare the reader the details of my voyage and of my life on board ship, and shall merely state that there were annoyances in plenty, both as regards the accommodation for the passengers and the conduct of the captain, whose sobriety was more than doubtful.' "

"But here's the real find," Marghie said. She handed him a black-and-white marbled composition book. In the flyleaf Danny had written:

THE BOOK OF GETTING EVEN

On page two were further specimens of his mirror-writing. Held up to the light, the pages seemed to report on Indo-Chinese exploits alongside Mouhot. "Henri and I" was the recurrent phrase. Together they had entered the pagoda at Mount Phrabat where the footprint of Gautama the Buddha is preserved, prowled the ruins at Ayutha, paid their respects to the Lion Rock at the port of Chantaboun, bivouacked in the forests of Laos, become lovers at an Annamite mission in the Ko-Man Islands, observed monkeys teasing a crocodile along the river at Paknam-Ven. Danny referred to himself and Mouhot (note the order) as "co-discoverers" of Angkor. He told how at Luang Prabang, on a hillock overlooking the Khan River, he'd buried Mouhot with his own hands and heaped up a tomb. Still holding the pages to the light, Marghie read on: "One of these temples — a rival to that of Solomon, and erected by some ancient Michael Angelo — might take an honorable place beside our most beautiful buildings. It is grander than anything left to us by Greece or Rome, and presents a sad contrast to the state of barbarism in which the nation is now plunged." On a fresh page, also mirror-written, was the following:

> *Excellency!*
> *You who call yourself "physician to sick governments throughout the world" had better listen to me, you blood-soaked ghoul, you fawning piece of shit!*
> *Item: In the fall of '68, before seizing power, you destabilized the Paris Peace Talks with secret promises to the North of a*

better deal if they waited for your scoundrel to be elected. And by how many years did you prolong that war, once you came to power? And how many additional American deaths did you preside over? I'LL TELL YOU, YOU BASTARD! 20,552! And how many Vietnamese? Half a million? Three quarters of a million? These were real people, see? THEY LIKED BREATHING THE AIR IN AND OUT AS MUCH AS YOU!

Item: You lent the full weight of our support, in 1971, to Pakistani generals' massacres of civilians in East Bengal and their attack on India launched from West Pakistan.

Item: You murdered Salvador Allende.

Item: You encouraged armed Kurdish insurrection in Northern Iraq with no intention of allowing them to win. When they'd served your geopolitical purpose, you cut off the aid and hung them out to dry.

Item: You incited goons of yours, the Indonesian Armed forces, armed with American-made weapons, to commit wholesale genocide against the people of East Timor.

Item: You incited Zaireans to invade Angola, then quietly gave the signal for South Africa to intervene against them.

Item: YOU KILLED THE CAMBODIAN NATION. THIS, EXCELLENCY, WAS YOUR CHEF D'OEUVRE. KNOW WHY I CAN'T STAND BEING JEWISH ANYMORE? BECAUSE YOU ARE!

I HAVE DONE MY HOMEWORK, YOUR GRACE. I HAVE SEARCHED OUT YOUR CRIMES AND WEIGHED THEM IN THE SCALES OF JUSTICE. AND I KNOW THIS, HARVARD BOY: YOU ARE THE MASTERMIND OF DEATH IN OUR TIME. YOU ARE THE GREAT ANNIHILATOR.

I AM, SIR, AS SIMPLE AS A FLAME. THEREFORE,

*FEAR ME. ON BEHALF OF THE VIETNAMESE
PEOPLE, THE LAOTIAN PEOPLE, THE BENGALIS,
THE CHILEANS, THE KURDS, THE EAST
TIMORESE, THE ANGOLANS, I DECREE THAT YOU
SHALL NO LONGER ENCUMBER THE EARTH.
AND ON BEHALF OF THE CAMBODIAN PEOPLE,
MR. AMERICAN METTERNICH, I SHALL PISS ON
YOUR STINKING CORPSE!*
  Very truly yours,
  Daniel L. Hundert

The birds were singing. A mist hung on the lake. At the other
end of the hall, Grisha and Lilo stirred in their room. A window
could be heard to open. Lilo called out: "Franush! Get in this house!
Franush Hundert? Franush!" Marghie and Gabriel spoke low.

He said, "Makes me queasy to look at backwards writing."

She said, "All my life the men, at ten-minute intervals, have
tended to start speaking what sounds like Urdu — but you know
what it is? It's politics. It's votes and wars and far countries and the
rest. And every mother's son seems to go for it. Oh, Gabe, couldn't
we do without all these politics? This is the first real peep out of
Danny in seven years, and it's politics. I had hoped for something
better from all that silence. I had hoped he'd pass on a little
illumination, not just one more tirade about international affairs.
I'm disappointed."

Danny's letter to the esteemed former secretary, now a well-
fed lion of New York society and very highly paid consultant to
multinational corporations, was for Gabriel, if not for her, easy
enough to follow. Turning the page he found this, not in reverse,
to confirm his fears:

I WILL WRITE NO MORE.

And, indeed, the rest of the notebook was blank. He told her what he thought the last words meant. "Emphasis falls on 'write.' 'I will *write* no more.' See?"

"Let's not show Mom and Dad."

"No. What would be the point?"

"What can we do?"

"Sit and wait."

They hadn't long. Marghie occupied herself with the kitchen garden she and Danny had laid out the summer between their freshman and sophomore years. The asparagus bed they'd prayed over and despaired of had worked with a will for several seasons now. But what a riot the rest was. Lilo had planted it, then neglected it. Tomatoes needed staking, radishes rotted in the ground, zucchinis grew too large for eating, kale ran to seed. Cursing, Marghie put her head down and strove to bring the garden back.

Her "baby" was with her, perpetually eighteen-months-old and perpetually good. Slept like a top, at a little remove. She'd glance up every now and then to check on him. Here in the garden, for only her to see, was her biggest secret. Gabriel had let fall one day that his best companion was imaginary, always had been, that he was really never alone, was always turning in solitude to the apparition beside him. And she'd exclaimed about the baby boy she gave birth to in fourth grade and had mothered ever since. "Even Danny doesn't know." Turned out that both spent their richest hours in the company of nonexistent beings, loving them supremely. Marghie had been to the sperm bank, had browsed through the catalogs of donors. "I just didn't see anyone I really liked," she told Gabriel, and decided to stick to her "baby."

This morning he'd swum out far and was diving for weeds. He pierced head-first the ever-colder layers of water, reaching blindly, not knowing what the depth was. When the pressure got too strong and the cold too sharp he turned for the light. A scowling carp flashed up and veered from him. Gabriel broke the surface, drank the air. For swimming, this limpid little lake was greatly preferable to Pontchartrain, which he'd last been in at night. A bath in warm ink, it had seemed. You dreaded to put your head under. You swam high in the water. An inadvertent mouthful made you gag. But these Wisconsin waters were an absolution. He shivered and swam. Expelling the air all at once from his lungs, he sank to greener depths. Now his feet entered a yielding, chinchilla-like element. He gave a kick, rose and rose and, lungs bursting, broke the surface with a shout.

He had a number in mind, a ten followed by an exponent of ten, raised by a factor of twelve. It was the biggest number he'd ever thought of, equivalent to a one followed by a trillion zeros. To print it would require, he guessed, about three hundred million pages. Ten to the tenth to the twelfth — this was a *really* big number, and Gabriel knew in the instant (without knowing how he knew) what this number was. It was the radius of the universe, the whole not just the observable universe, and it cleared up a couple of things — the flatness problem, that the universe is close to critical density, poised on a knife's edge between eternal expansion and eventual collapse; and the horizon problem, that the universe is homogeneous and isotropic over distances too large for information to have traveled since the Big Bang.

Underwater was where he could be most himself, and he'd have dived again despite itching palms and chattering teeth had not Lilo on the jetty waved him in. A couple of strangers flanked her, men in suits. They showed medallions and said the house would be searched, a federal warrant having been issued. They spoke mainly in the passive voice. Blue-lipped, trembling under his towel, Gabriel answered questions. Faced with authority he found himself, to his mortification, inclining their way. Oh, to be back in the icy water. When was the last time he had seen or communicated with Daniel

Laszlo Hundert? Were any effects of said person in his possession? Did he have knowledge of said person's recent whereabouts prior to yesterday evening? Did he have knowledge of said person's movements yesterday? Was he aware that said person had been apprehended in the state of Maine following an incident yesterday evening?

This was not the kind of house in which radios or televisions were turned on or newspapers read. Nobody here knew what had been afoot in the great world. But on Mount Desert Island, at the head of Somes Sound, in the rock-ribbed village of Northeast Harbor, from about seven forty-five in the evening, what had been afoot was Danny, the FBI informed them now. Daniel Laszlo Hundert had trespassed onto the grounds of the former secretary's summer retreat. It was all Gabriel had to hear to know suddenly the whole chronicle, behold it as if at the movies . . . Danny hiding till nightfall behind a beauty bush in flower at the edge of the property; watching as room by room the lights come on in the stately house, watching the sea-green shutters darken to black and the white clapboards to evening blue. Guests begin arriving for dinner. (This Danny hasn't foreseen.) He hears car doors slam and pea stone underfoot, and the pleasing laughter of women. Carried downhill on the breeze is even a whiff of somebody's perfume. He loads his gun, a revolver purchased at a pawn shop. He takes out a handkerchief and cleans his glasses. And now he charges the house shouting, "In the name of the Cambodian people!" — his first outcry after all these years. Security emerges from a potting shed off the main house. They follow procedure, ordering him to halt and throw his weapon toward them. Danny zigzags up the rise. They fire over his head. Danny crouches but keeps moving. And now he shoots, hitting first a chimney, then a weather vane, then a dormer window. It is not until he is on the back terrace that security fires for his legs.

The Mount Desert police had responded. They'd alerted the

Bangor offices of the FBI. An ambulance had taken Danny to Bar Harbor. The dinner party in Northeast went on as planned . . .

He had one leg shattered at the knee and the other pierced through at the calf. This much the feds could tell them. No, he would not die. Yes, he was under indictment. Yes, he had legal representation, assigned by the court. No, he hadn't entered a plea; had refused, in fact, to say a word.

There were four or five more men inside, ransacking. Lilo, Grisha, and Marghie stood together under the oaks. Elise and Ned had come frantically from their house, but stood off at the edge of the meadow, judging that the respectful distance to keep. The Hunderts looked like people look when moment-by-moment assurances are shorn away. They looked like what they were — displaced persons, unhoused from their lives. Joining the broken circle under the trees, Gabriel found his arms were wide enough to hold all three of them.

What a pregnant item of news! Paris, Moscow, Beijing buzzed with it. From Plains, Georgia, where they were on holiday, President and Mrs. Jimmy Carter communicated their concern to the former secretary. Abe Rosenthal, that old phrasemaker, called the case of Daniel Hundert an American tragedy. Barbara Walters worked her usual *haimischer* angle — how heartbreaking for those poor nice distinguished parents. Paul Harvey declared that with this pathetic attempt at political murder Daniel Hundert had brought the sixties to a close. Lately paroled after serving time for statutory rape, Al Capp conceived of a new character, Spoily Brattert, who preaches peace and carries a piece and cries his mealy eyes out when they cart him off to the hoosegow. Midge Decter cooked up majorful reflections for the next *Commentary*. And Gore Vidal declared all over the Hollywood Hills and the Amalfi coast that this Jewboy in glasses had been wrong for the job.

———

Hyde Park. November 1979. Gabriel Geismar — lately Associate Professor of Astrophysics Gabriel Geismar — ate grilled cheese in a window booth at Flavio's while outside the devil beat his wife. Common enough at this season, but now, with the sun shining still, rain turned to snow. A peal of thunder lingered out.

From the window he spotted Lilo and Grisha at the corner, holding hands. At that distance, they seemed to be laughing. He hadn't seen them hold hands like that before, like sweethearts. As they got closer he saw that they weren't laughing; they were crying, openly, looking neither left nor right, just busy crying. The sun and snow came down on them. As they passed Flavio's, Gabriel could tell something from their faces: that Lilo knew why she was crying but Grisha did not, that she cried for good reason but he cried only because she did, that everything baffled him now.

The public facts that week were these: Klansmen in Greensboro, North Carolina, shot to death four members of the Workers' Viewpoint Organization, an underground Maoist group; sixty-six Americans were taken hostage in Teheran; Father Coughlin died in Bloomfield Hills, Michigan; refugees from the People's Republic of Kampuchea gathered in vast numbers at the Thai border as fighting between Vietnamese and Khmer Rouge forces spread and harvests failed; and in Bangor, Maine, Daniel Hundert, having been declared mentally unfit to stand trial, was remanded for an indefinite period to the care of the federal penitentiary in Danbury, Connecticut.

After a moment of sitting still, loathing himself for the disinclination and feeling disinclined all the same, wanting only to stay in the warmth of Flavio's, Gabriel paid the check and went after Lilo and Grisha, striding to catch up to them.

"Lilo!"

Turning, she wiped away tears. Grisha did the same, seeing her do so. "Come up for tea," she said, embarrassed. And "Come up for tea," echoed Grisha. She turned on him, said something in Hungarian. He hung his head like a child.

"You must have gotten in last night," Gabriel said to her.

"I did. I got to see him before he was remanded. At least it's happened. At least we know now. I don't think release is ever very likely, do you? I know I could take care of him. I told the judge I could." During the four days in Bangor, she'd left Grisha with Marghie, who called promptly to say, "Get back as soon as you can. He wants you. He's being bad. Mom, who are Dritta and Drina? Who's Nicu? He keeps asking for them. He gets belligerent when I say I don't know anybody by those names. He tells me I'm a liar. He called me a *whore*, of all things. There's a laugh. You saw Danny?" But Lilo had hung up.

The apartment was airless. The steam heat banged. When they had their coats off, Grisha stared blackly at the radiator till it stopped, then went to the record player, put something on. He sat down in his usual chair, lapsed into leonine blankness.

"The neighbors above pound on their floor," said Lilo. "The neighbors below pound on their ceiling. They're tired of act three of *Falstaff*." It seemed this was all Grisha listened to anymore. His encyclopedic love of opera had refined itself to this: *Una, due, tre, quattro, cinque, sei, sette botte, otto, nove, dieci, undici, dodeci. Mezzanotte.* When the park at Windsor is lit up by the moon, and you stand beside Herne's great oak and feel the heavy ridiculous antlers on your head, and pull your cloak closer and hear the chimes of midnight ringing out (and the illimitable audience, unseen beyond the footlights, rustling with glee), then you know that life is as mocking as this: imps, elves, sprites, goblins, bats, and flies do their worst — nip, prick, pinch, sting, and bite. The good deeds a man has done do not defend him. Here is the *burla*, the jest, *the last act*! sing the demons, reveling. In this your midnight they have spattered you with mire.

———

Late spring, 1980. New Orleans. 3:30 A.M. "Hello?"

"It's me."

"Marg, do you know what time it is?"

"Gabe, there's something I've been meaning to tell you —"

"I'm sleeping."

"— for ever so long."

"You can tell me but I'm sleeping. I won't remember."

"Oh, you'll remember this. This will sink down deep. It's about a Siamese prince and a girl from Kiev. And it's one-hundred-percent true, unlike some of your stories, Gabe. Hope Dan never told you."

"No."

"Good. It was always Danny's special request. Dad used to tell us. There was a prince of Siam who came all the way to Oxford for college. But he had a mortal fear of boats, this prince, so he had to travel overland. On the way home one time, passing through Kiev, he came down with pneumonia. The tsar's doctors were sent to attend him and he got better, and when he was nearly well he went out to a ball where he saw the most beautiful girl in all of Russia. And he fell for her and married her and took her home to Bangkok. His father died and his eldest brother became king."

"This is getting kind of shaggy, Marg."

"Wait, wait. Then the eldest died, and the number-two son got to be king. Then he died too, and the number-three son, the one who'd brought the girl back from Kiev, got to be King. And this meant a girl from Kiev was now Queen of Siam!"

"That's some story."

"It's not over yet. Everybody in Bangkok *hated* her. When she decreed the electrification of the palace they couldn't stand any more. They started grinding up the lightbulbs and putting them in her food. And in a few weeks she dropped dead of an intestinal hemorrhage. You still there?"

"Say what? I must have dozed."

"She wanted lightbulbs."

"What?"

"They gave her lightbulbs."

"What?"

"Goodnight, Gabey."

Next morning, lying awake in his old bedroom on Terpsichore, all of this had turned to murk in his head. Something about Bangkok. Something about Kiev. There were the duties of the day to consider. There was a lot of sifting to do. Keep this. Throw that out. Six nights ago, his mother had been with Pearl and Maurice Kaufman at Galatoire's for Pearl's birthday. A big table of friends. Plenty of laughs. Indeed, Maury had said something so funny it caused Rowena to laugh till she couldn't catch her breath, then to sneeze, sneeze again, sneeze a third time, and at the fourth sneeze to slump forward. She made no fuss. A perfect lady, dead where she sat. They spread her out, of course, and called the medics. An ophthalmologist from the next table pounded on her chest. What for? Rowena had picked her moment and was gone. A terrible night for all concerned. A terrible night for Galatoire's. But Gabriel felt his mother had masterminded this finish. "WIDOWED REBBITZIN DEAD OF THROMBOSIS AT GALATOIRE'S" — what a lead for the local Jewish weekly! The old man must have spun in his tomb.

Forsake what you want. Forsake science for religion or religion for science. Forsake eating meat, fish. Forsake going to work. Forsake friends, music, art, books, movies. Forsake sex, love. Forsake money. The only thing you cannot forsake is having been a child. Gabriel had caught the earliest flight out of O'Hare. On his own, without panic, without dread even, he had seen to the funeral and the laying to rest beside Milt. This noon, in a somehow rapturous mood, he remembered a headline from the previous fall — "Ike and Mamie, Together Again." And remembered Mrs. E's declaration that Ike fought the wars and she turned the lamb chops. Gabriel told himself, *Milt and Rowena did their jobs*, and told himself, *I did mine.* (Ike and Mamie he couldn't vouch for but, given his lightheartedness, would grant them every benefit of the doubt.)

Now he took himself to lunch at the fatal restaurant. Seated, the starched napkin spread on his lap, he fell to contemplating a very elderly couple, fresh from Sunday Mass, at the next table. They were lifting martinis nearly as big as they were. "To you, dollin," said man to wife. Gabriel ordered one of his own. He wasn't in the habit of drinking such things even in the evening, much less at lunch. They'd carry him out on a stretcher if he did. He took only a symbolic sip after raising the glass and saying, inwardly, *To you, man and wife.* Then he threw the final shibboleth to the winds. He ordered and scarfed down a dozen of Galatoire's finest on the half shell. And drank the oyster liquor. "Beyond praise," he told the management.

Back on Terpsichore was a house to deconsecrate. Gabriel found photographs of himself at every stage of development, all of his report cards from kindergarten to twelfth, all of his merit badges from summer camp. His first pair of shoes, bronzed, were there. A cookie tin that rattled when he shook it turned out to contain his baby teeth. His prize-winning science fair projects, somewhat mangled, were there. Every letter he'd ever written home was there.

All the while he'd thought they were heaping him, overwhelming him, it was he who'd heaped them. His *archivists* is what they'd been, protecting all this stuff. But what of before he'd come along? Here, from young married days, was a photo. Milt is handsome, built. Rowena appears witty and brave. They've got on the swimming costumes of yesteryear and are lounging by a pool. To you, man and wife. Verso she's written "Havana de Cuba, 1951." Here's another — he in a dinner jacket, she bare-shouldered in tulle. They look like movie stars! And another — Milt in naval uniform; on the back he's written "Manila, on leave." Gabriel saw spots. He recollected a movie Marghie had subjected him to a few winters back, *Stage Door Canteen*, a morale booster from the early forties. "The great Borzage," she'd declared, auteurist to the end, as they settled down to watch it. Fifteen minutes in, Gabriel said, "Seems like a propaganda film to me."

"I forbid you to call it that. All the wisdom of the world is in this picture." It concerned one of those dance halls set up for servicemen. You fox trotted or jitterbugged with volunteer girls whose last names you couldn't ask. No making dates for after hours; they picked up your pass if you tried. All designed to get the boys back to the base or the ship without the customary dose of syphilis or gonorrhea.

As an alternative to whoring, such dens of abstinence had proved a pretty thin draw. The purpose of *Stage Door Canteen* was to persuade the fellows to give them a try. And the canteen of the movie is interesting, to say the least. Katharine Cornell, Lynne Fontanne, and Gypsy Rose Lee are waitresses. Hostesses include Martha Scott, Helen Hayes, Judith Anderson, Ina Claire, Merle Oberon, and Dame May Whitty. Paul Muni, Ray Bolger, Alfred Lunt, George Jessel, Johnny Weismuller, and Sam Jaffe are busboys. Ed Wynn's the coat-check girl. Harpo Marx chases everything in a skirt.

"Lot of highly perishable humor in this, Marg. Forties humor."

"You wait."

Ethel Waters sings "Quicksand," accompanied by Count Basie. Benny Goodman does prodigies on the licorice stick. All the big bands are there: Cugat's, Kay Kyser's, Lombardo's, Freddie Martin's. *"We'll be singing, Hallelujah! — marching through Berlin!"* crows Merman.

"If you could be any woman, girls, what woman would you be?" Elsa Maxwell asks the room, and Gypsy Rose Lee roars back, "Hitler's *widow!*"

Gracie Fields sings the Lord's Prayer. Kate Hepburn, all Yankee bluntness, warns of sacrifices and heartbreak ahead. Yehudi Menuhin plays Schubert's "Ave Maria."

"Swell fella, Tallulah!" says a navy man. "Not too bad yourself!" Tallulah answers with a look at the guy's wide shoulders.

"Lot of unrationed ham, Marg."

"Wait'll this thing breaks your heart." She scooched down in her seat. "You'll think you're back *in* the forties. Let's pretend we are. Let's pretend we haven't even been born yet."

Lanny Ross sings a four-handkerchief song about lovers forced to part: *In dreams, we'll always be together, beneath the moonlit sky, we mustn't say goodbye.* A boy and girl, newly met, take each other by the hand. *Each night, I'll push aside the mountains, I'll drain the ocean dry.* War emotions grip the canteen. *We mustn't say goodbye.*

"Where was your father in the war anyway?" Marghie asked.

"Mindanao. And a lot of time at sea. Chaplain on a battleship for a while. I don't know much about it, really."

"Then how come you know everything about our father?"

Remembered now, here amid the leavings of his parents' lives, her question belatedly pierced him. Why, indeed? Why did Gregor and Lilo Hundert merit his rapt study while Milton and Rowena Geismar went to the sour-apple heap? Or had he been studying Milton and Rowena all along? Had this furious craving for other, nobler origins been only a blind? He fancied he'd been ridding himself of those two. But had he been exalting them — his own father, the bravest of men, his own mother, the dearest of women — by means of a substitution? Questions like these ring down the curtain on family romance. Lilo and Grisha threw off their masks. And guess who, greatly loved, greatly loved, were hiding humbly underneath. A week later he finished the sorting, put the house on the market, walked out the front door for the last time. And went home — for that's what he'd learned to call it — to Chicago.

————

Gabriel had thought he grasped the blood secret of the Hunderts — to ride your obsession till the road runs out, then ride on into open fields, hollows, thickets so dense day cannot be told there from night. Then he found out something more. He and Lilo had been up to the Loop for dinner and were strolling south on Michigan Avenue. It was autumn, the breeze off the lake was mild. "Heavenly when it decides to be," she said. They stopped in front of the Art Institute. "Let's sit for a while, it's so pleasant here. I've another couple of hours before the evening nurse goes off." She had something uneasy to tell him, he could see. "I've decided" — she hung fire — "decided to give up the house in Portage. It's just not manageable any more. When I called Ellie and Ned to tell them, we had a good jag. It helped."

"I just can't imagine anyone else in that house."

"Oh, there won't be. Ellie said she couldn't bear that. Said it will stand empty in remembrance. That was when we all broke down."

Nothing more to say. Then Gabriel: "Marghie told me how she and Grisha used to come here on Saturdays, just the two of them."

"Every Saturday."

"And Danny?"

"Danny and I would do something else. We were more varied.

The Field Museum, the aquarium, occasionally up to the Lincoln Park Zoo. But Grisha and Marghie had their strict routine."

"She told me they would go for egg-drop soup and shrimp toast at the Emperor's Choice."

"Sometimes barbequed spare ribs."

"And that then they would go to a barber shop near South Ingleside where Grisha would get a shoeshine. And then they would go to a florist on East Fifty-fifth and get Marg a flower for her dress."

"She never came home without a flower."

"And then they'd head up here to the Art Institute. And that was the Saturday drill."

A professional dog walker came past with a company of eight or ten, all sizes and shapes, each on its own leash. "Look at that," she said. "Perfect accord. Because there's no religion involved, don't you think?" She looked mortally tired. "Somewhere, surely, are girls who love their mothers."

"It happens. And boys who love their fathers. I think the problem starts with men who look at their sons and say, 'Why aren't you more like me?'"

"Or women who look at their daughters and say it. You weren't going to add that, because you know I'm such a mother. This really is what I always wonder. Why is she not more like me? Grisha used to say, 'He is yours and she is mine.' I used to say, 'Grisha, they are changelings, the both of them.' . . . There is a thing I would like for you to do. A very great favor. Oh, not right away. Maybe years from now, or sooner. Before I ask, there is something you must know, which Marghie and Danny do not. Grisha had a child before he met me. About fifteen years before."

"Fifteen? Is it possible?"

"Just. He was thirty when we met. He'd fathered a daughter when he was fifteen. The mother was somewhere in her twenties, perhaps twenty-seven or twenty-eight." Lilo sat there on the steps, her knees drawn up under her chin, fingering the pleats of her skirt, shivering a little. "She was Rom, you see, a very nice woman who happened to fall in love with a teenage boy she saw crossing City Park from the Minta each afternoon. And she asked him to her room in the northern district, and he said no, and she asked him again, and he said yes. Then he didn't see her anymore for a long time. When he did, a year or so later, she had a fair-skinned baby with her and she said, 'Look at my Jewish Gypsy!' And Grisha ran away. Poor boy, can you imagine? Would she go to his parents? To his school? Would she ruin him? Wasn't the baby as likely someone else's? He agonized, but Dritta did nothing — Dritta was her name. She only presented herself and the child, from time to time, for him to see. Gradually he overcame his fear enough to talk to her. He learned the little girl's name — Drina. He asked if she had money enough for the two of them. She had what she begged. He asked if the child had enough to eat. Enough, but had been quite sick over the winter. Dritta's brother, who played cimbalom in a restaurant, gave her a bit of money. The rest of the family had cut her off completely. Grisha kept contact with them through the twenties. Sent money from Leipzig where he was at university. Dritta could not read or write, so it wasn't easy for her to acknowledge. And suddenly the deutschmark had no value and there was no point in sending it. When later on the new mark was established, he sent to her again. After he got to the States in the midthirties, he would send dollars, but could only guess whether they were reaching her and the child, a teenager by then. When his colleagues asked why he was putting currency through the mails, he'd say, 'Oh, sending a little cash to family of mine.' A letter in thirty-nine announced a new mouth to feed. Drina had had a little boy. Nicu. Then the war came. Hungary stayed out for almost two years, a complicated story. But no more mail got through to us.

"That little boy. Danny and Marghie's — what? Nephew, I guess, older than they were. Grisha a grandfather at thirty-one. Think of that."

"Among Gypsies there are stranger genealogical anomalies. In the spring of forty-four the war came in earnest to Hungary. It seems Dritta and Drina and the child had been forced out to the countryside. We learned all this from letters that arrived only after the war. Dritta had given them to a peasant family she trusted would try to forward them when they could. The extraordinary thing was, they did. A package arrived on our doorstep in late forty-five. Some of the letters are dictated by Dritta in Hungarian, others in Romanian, depending on which language the letter writer was best at, I suppose, and with occasional bits of Romany mixed in. For many years now I have known them by heart, even the uninterpretable bits. The Gypsies unlike the Jews had absolutely no grounds for hope, or delusion rather, before the war came in forty-four, about their prospects in Hungary. Dritta's final letter was written from a village about a hundred kilometers south of Budapest. October of forty-four. Hitler had forced Horty out and put Szálasi in, and the SS and Arrow Cross got busy. It was the last act, and they knew it. They would lose the war against the Allies but win their war against the Jews and the Roma."

A hook-and-ladder came wailing past. Doppler effect. Lilo paused.

"Her last letter said, 'Drina and Nicu have gone to the river.' We wondered a while and then we knew what we knew. It is not so easy to drown yourself, not so easy to drown a five-year-old child. Drina did it. We found that much out from the people who'd sent us the letters. Can you imagine? The stranger to yourself you'd need to become, the strength of the little boy struggling to escape you. Very few people could possibly . . . You hang on to your shred of hope, your abundance of delusion, till it's too late. It is simply too hard to believe the executioner is waiting for you and your child. But Drina saw the worst and had no room for doubt. So she wanted to deny *them* the victory. I have never for one day ceased to think of this. It was a long, long time before Grisha and I could speak about having children of our own. 'I have been a father and a grandfather already,' he would say."

Lilo smiled her best confiding smile, and all the punishing years were on her. "Ten years together, and no baby. But then —" she broke off.

But then in the fall of forty-eight she was pregnant, and the following summer a boy and girl were born. The rest you know, more or less. The raising up and casting down of the Hunderts in their time. She laid a hand on Gabriel's and her head on his shoulder and told him what the very big favor was, the duty he must do.

———

Days pass, weeks. She comes home with groceries and the *Chicago Tribune*. She pays the day nurse her wages, bids her goodnight. She wants to rest for a minute. For just thirty seconds. She comes into the living room, takes her usual seat beside Grisha. He gives her his empty lion stare. She's taken to giving it back to him. He has turned to her in bed the previous night, saying, "My wife is not here. She has gone to visit her family. I think you should sleep in the other room." Lilo told him she was comfortable where she was. He moved to the edge of the bed, then came back to give her hand a squeeze, her cheek a kiss.

Where is that newspaper? Left on the kitchen counter. Oh, she is too tired anyhow for news, too tired for anything new at all.

For anything but the old high thing, the love of the dead. "Then let us be among them." The peremptory, reasonless ardor to live admits of intermittences. These are dangerous. A freedom has germinated and grown in Lilo Hundert — unsayable, but she's treasured up six prescriptions of Elavil, enough for both of them, so as to know with certainty that they can go, make a reasonable exit, when the time is right. Delicious that an antidepressant in sufficient quantity grants the ticket out.

She puts it in their tea. She hasn't known till she does so that she's going to. Today is inexplicably the day. They'll find us in our chairs, properly dressed. This is best. She sets out a very large dish of dry food for Franush, and a big bowl of water. She resumes her seat beside Grisha. They drink. She clears her head of everything. He nods. She takes his hand. His head is down. Quite a long time passes, it seems. "Finish, Grisha." He finishes. A long time passes.

Then it happens. In a blaze she remembers — everything. She has only to regret that Grisha is denied this. Her conclusion is all that concluding ought to be, she decides, her luck the greatest luck. To die of everything and everything all at once. *In battle, in forests* . . . She puts her feet up, gets comfortable . . . *at the precipice of the mountains, on the dark gray sea, in the midst of javelins and arrows. . .* A few words more and she'll have made her devotion . . . *in sleep, in confusion, in the depths of shame* . . .

But tonight the words are breathtaking.

————

"Mighty thoughtful of them to name the town after him," says Marghie, her usual line. She and Gabriel are on Metro-North out of Grand Central Terminal, in transit, as on the first Sunday of every month, to the federal correctional facility at Danbury. They typically get the earliest flight from O'Hare to LaGuardia and take the last one back, with a lot of cab- and train-catching in between. It makes for a long day. On Metro-North this noon she's been reminiscing, between Wilton and Cannondale, about another set of twins at the Lab School, one year younger than themselves, who were so stricken with jealousy of her and Danny's Hungarian that they'd developed a twintalk of their own, a Katzenjammerese based on putting the syllable *ob* before any vowel or vowel cluster. "Greg and Lainey Steinmetz."

"Greg and Lainey invented that? Right there at the Lab School?"

"They did."

"Wise up, sister. There were kids at New Orleans Country Day who spoke *ob* like nobody's business. Who knows who invented it? Maybe some guy whose name is lost to glory. Maybe, as with calculus and evolution, two geniuses working independently of each other. I'm a dab hand at *ob* myself. 'Obi mobust sobearch thobe hobeavobens fobor whobat obis dobenobied mobe obon obearth.' That's Einstein."

He opens the schedule and reads aloud the remaining stations: "Cannondale, Branchville, Reading, Bethel, Danbury." Both recall their brilliance of yesteryear. Like a husband who's not proposed love in many a moon, he shyly says, "Shall we have a go?" But she shrugs and shakes her head. He knows his heart wouldn't be in it either.

Louise and Baby June have passed away. The Lampion is closed now. On the final night of business, a winter ago, Marghie had run her all-time favorite, *Rules of the Game*. A bitter evening, sleet coming in sideways, last month's snow piled up and blackened at the curbsides, floes in the lake and the river. An audience of about four. She lit the marquee, popped the corn, rolled the film. Gabriel sat with her, as usual, outside the projection booth. They held hands while, on screen, life purported to be no more serious than a country weekend, complication washing harmlessly off of everyone, even the dead man in the garden. A fine, sepia-toned print. The gargantuan lady pianist says, "You're looking thin!" to all and sundry, and warns of a hard winter coming. Everybody's under a spell, it

seems, miserable with longing, a step away from bliss. New loves
are confessed, marriages totter, fistfights erupt, shots ring out. The
stakes are mortal in this game nobody can decipher the rules of, the
opera buffa in earnest; all play-act from a libretto none has read. "A
chill's on the air," says the marquis. "Come in or catch your death."
As she closed up shop forever, Marghie's praise ran on. "Greatest
of filmmakers. Tells what life is like. You laugh till you cry, that's
what. Then maybe you get to laugh again."

Gabriel feels there's got to be a statute of limitations on
intergenerational rancor. He's all for "coming to terms," as they say,
whatever exactly it means, and preached coming to terms to Marghie
when the impossible news broke on them. It did not take. No statute
of limitations for her. She alone would tend to her mother's ashes,
she announced following the cremations, and took what was left
of Lilo Hundert formally, solemnly, ceremoniously, sacramentally,
majestically to the dump, along with fourteen boxes of research for
a book never completed. "To punish her," she said, shining with
rage, "for the murder of my father." Franush she dropped off at the
ASPCA. "I can't have that wild thing around here. Nothing at all
like my old girls." Gabriel went straight to the animal shelter and
adopted Franush, whom he doesn't like much either. He called
Marghie unforgivable for this outrage, and for the ashes, and for the
manuscript (but finds he does forgive, as she is all the family he's got).
Lately she eats eggs, cheese, even a little fish, and has filled out. She's
been doing some film reviews on local radio. Even old people who
never go to the movies say they enjoy her. She's getting a bobcat
reputation. She's been asked to write for one of the national slicks.
Some say she'll be big. Still lives on Halsted, still hopes to meet the
right guy, still calls herself happy.

Danny lives, forevermore, in the criminal madhouse. He lives
also in the minor historical footnotes among those who, so as not
to fall out of history, so as to be safe in its fold, have attempted,

from loneliest impulse, a single definitive act. To get even. With the big perpetrators. To roil the sleep of the mighty. One of his legs is healing fine, the other isn't. He is not allowed to have crutches or a walker, or his glasses, after having tried to swallow them. And all he'd wanted was to join the cavalcade of the large deeds, like Dad. Because he'd liked his father's line, the history-making business, because he wanted in on the act. But Dad is with Oppenheimer and Fermi. Danny is with Sara Jane Moore and Lynette "Squeaky" Fromme — warehoused like them at federal expense.

Danny lives also, and most intensively, at Angkor. As on a tablet half-effaced, the names of the dead are still partially in him. But over the names he has inscribed the undulatory reliefs of the temples at Angkor. He has taken them from a picture book and given to laterite and sandstone the safekeeping of his head. Danny the memorious has Preah Ko, Banteay Srei, Ta Keo, Baphuon, Angkor Wat, and Angkor Tom in him. All night he wanders the void avenues and empty causeways, through moonlit arches and shadowed colonnades. From a thousand towers the face of Lokeshvara smiles down vaguely. Danny spreads his arms and says to no one in particular, for he is alone in the fervid dream, that New York, Chicago, Los Angeles must come to this: forests growing up over them, devouring them, one day millennia hence to be hewn down and the lovely places beheld again.

"Think he'll talk today?" she asks.

"I think he'll just do his usual smiling. You know what I'm afraid of? That he'll smile when we tell him what's happened. I must say, frankly, that I agree with a tiny little graffito I saw, right under KEEP COOL, BUT CARE and to the left of FRODO LIVES, in a men's room over at the physics building. THE SILENCE OF DANIEL HUNDERT IS OVERRATED is what it says. It's faded out. Been there for some time. Think Danny wrote it?"

"No. I think you did."

"I most certainly did not!"

"You put it there."

"Maybe."

"You put it there."

"I did."

She stares a while out the window. "Con*neck*ticut," she murmurs. At the Danbury station, they catch a taxi. Visiting hours at the facility are from one to three, every Sunday, plus holidays. Security checks of visitors and their parcels begin at noon, though Gabriel and Marghie have brought nothing more than themselves, and their burden of news.

Danny wears the usual regulation jumpsuit. His haircut is military. Waiving off an attendant, he rolls his wheelchair to the table. He is clean shaven today, brutally so; an angry rash mottles his neck and cheeks. Since their last visit the laces have been taken out of his shoes, Gabriel notices, and notices, too, how denuded he looks without glasses.

Danny reaches across the table for each of them. "You may not touch," says the attendant, as always. He draws back. Dan is all obedience now, he is whipped, wears a sealed-up look telling neither of fear nor hope. He is the still center of the cyclone he has raised. He turns on the attendant a stare of Christ-like forbearance that could go on forever but for Marghie saying,

"*Anyám apám meghaltak.*" Mom and Dad are dead. "She killed him, him and herself."

Gabriel feels he has rights, even at this moment, feels he is of their clay. "She wanted to let him go," he says. "And she didn't want to live without —"

"She killed him," says Marghie, unappeasable. "If she weren't dead, I'd kill her. I'd like to kill her even though she is dead."

Danny looks hard at his sister, then at Gabriel. He does not, as feared, smile.

"Know what?" she continues. "I didn't cry." (A lie, a big one. She's been a voluptuous crier in private for years now.) "Crying's your department."

But he is parsecs past crying, Gabriel understands now. Danny breathes a comprehensive sigh. At the dead end of understanding, after a dozen or more of these monthly visits, Gabriel understands. Danny has wanted to suffer, suffer compassionately, get to the headwaters and source of all tears. He has wanted to enroll himself among the lost, take his rightful place there. And see? He has. Marghie puts a lightning kiss on the top of his head before the guard can object, and goes out, leaving Gabriel to make his own goodbye.

———

November, 1980. He hurries along Andrássy Street. Budapest, proud of its scars, gives him now and then a nod. "Parcel me out in one hundred parts" — such had been Grisha's directive in a will dating from the early sixties. He'd specified each of the locales where he should lie: in the third ring at the State Opera; under the arcade of the Dreschler Mansion; before the mural at the Zeneakadémia; in the palm house at the zoo; at the base of the statue of George Washington in Városliget. Such was the very big favor Lilo had sworn Gabriel to — this distribution of Grisha's ashes.

Today he makes only a start, depositing only the first handful, tied in a handkerchief. The rest is at the hotel, in a canister. Grisha is coming back. By the time Gabriel is through, Budapest will be full of him. Invisibly presiding. A crumb of Hundert Gregor in the crypt of the Matthias Church; at the base of the statue of Pallas Athena in Városhaz Road; in Ruszwurm Cukrászda, a pastry shop in Szentháromsag Road; along the escarpment of the Fisherman's Bastion; at the base of the statue of Lajos Kossuth; at the head of the Petőfi Bridge; in the courtyard of what had been the Minta.

The ashes have rested peaceably for a few months in his bedroom closet. He is lively now at the task of distributing them: a particle of the old man at the Premonstratensian Chapel in Margaret Island; under the seat of the funicular up Castle Hill; at the mouth of the Szemlő-hegy Cave; at the Great Synagogue in Tobacco Street; on Liberation Bridge; at the Óbuda Parish Church; on the graves of his parents at the Jewish Cemetery in Kozma Street; at the statue of Ignáz Semmelweis in Gyulai Pal Street; on the steps of the house where Szilárd grew up; in the courtyard of the apartment house where von Neumann lived as a young man; at the Erzsébet Lookout Tower; in Nagyret Meadow; at the tomb of Gül Baba the Dervish.

Next day, on to the Turkish baths, a fresh handful of Grisha in his pocket. He'd specified five sites: the Rudas, the Rác, the Király, the Csaszar, and the Lukács. As Gabriel crosses the Elizabeth Bridge, a stranger falls in with him. "You are going to Rudas."

"I am, yes."

"You are better off with person like me. Otherwise —" He draws a finger across his throat. Gabriel walks on faster.

"You are homosexual, I see," the man calls after him. The nerve of some people. "Homosexual is unwelcome at Rudas. Better at Király, better at Rác. For small consideration I am taking you. We go in taxi. You are paying." Small-eared, straight-nosed, he seems a thoroughbred of some kind but dispossessed, a potentate in rags. Perhaps it makes sense to have a guide. The guy speaks English, at any rate — with a certain flair, even.

"Is unusual thumb you have."

"Don't start with me, buster."

When they get in the taxi the driver, a bloodshot ruin of a man, stares with unconcealed revulsion. "Király!" commands the potentate. The driver turns away, hatred in the clench of his shoulders, and steps on it. "Most unhappy. Do you know why? He is not great lover of Roma. And I am Rom."

The article itself, then. A Gypsy.

"Eleven hundred year ago these Magyars are crossing Carpathians and coming to this basin. From where? From somewhere in Urals Mountains. I am not illiterate Rom. I am going to school. Simione Cici is my name. Under Socialist Republic I am going — English, Russian, physic, mathematic. So they come here from Urals Mountains and they say, 'Here is pretty basin. Not any more nomads. We are staying.' This is story of Magyars. Now, do you know story of Roma?"

"Someone who loved the Gypsies, and is dead now, told me a few of the facts."

"You will please not to say 'Gypsies.' "

"Roma."

"Roma, excellent, who take long road from India, starting also more than thousand years ago. We go many places. Turkey, Egypt, Spain, England, USA. In Hungary we are called 'New Magyars' by those coming before us. Hungarian looks at Rom and sees — himself. Maybe does not like so much what he sees."

They arrive at the Király. Despite a handsome tip, Gabriel gets no acknowledgement from the driver who as he eases out into traffic turns back to spit from the window. "Poor aim!" Simione Cici shouts after him.

The attendant inside shows them to separate changing booths and provides them with 'modesty wear' — little aprons for covering the genitals. "Ridiculous," says Gabriel. "I won't wear mine."

"Men will think you are prostitute," says the Gypsy.

"Let 'em. You wear yours if you want."

"I never wear."

"They'll think you're —"

"Prostitute. I *am* prostitute. But not for you. For you I am only guide."

Gabriel enters the changing room, undresses, takes the tied-up handkerchief from his pocket, unfastens it delicately, covers one hand with a dusting of Grisha. "Show me to the plunge, guide."

They step into the gloom. An octagonal pool, fed by springs nearby, is full of men gabbing, floating, napping. Through colored apertures the cupola lets in a muted light. Steam rises. Gabriel enters the water and, immersing the ash-covered hand, watches the particles come back to the surface and scatter off.

"Next bath, please," he says to his guide.

"You are paying?"

"I am paying."

"What is point, mister, of going from Turkish bath to Turkish bath?"

"I've got a duty to discharge."

At the Lukács they are barred from the medicinal pools — prescription bathing only — but the thermal waters are open. In the changing room, as Gabriel smears his hand, Simione, abreast now of the purpose of all this bathing, says, "You are putting dead man in baths of all Budapest. Do I approve?"

"Carbon I am putting. Where's the harm?"

On to the others now, even the Rudas, where homosexual man is reputedly unwelcome. They arrive and depart without incident.

The final errand is to the Rác, where homosexual man is welcome indeed. A molly house with a pool is evidently what it is. Gabriel undresses for the fifth time today, dusts his hand, is ready to plunge in. Simione says, "Here at Rác you are allowed to masturbate me." Gabriel considers the infamy of it. But are not the Gypsy's parts as good, as Budapestian a place to smear Grisha as the doorstep of the Great Synagogue, or the Danubius Fountain, or the sweet shop in Szentháromsag Road? What the hell? It's accomplished in a minute, this mingling of mighty opposites — carbon, the outcome of life, and sperm, the precursor. Shame? Profanation? Gabriel feels as blameless as the lamb.

"Twenty-thousand forints, please," says Simione Cici.

————

It is no small thing he's done, waving four parents out of the station. He likes to picture them down the line, convened forever at the best table of the best dining car of the best train, with pink tablecloths and white roses and cut-glass goblets taking the light — Lilo and Milt and Rowena and Grisha getting better acquainted for all of eternity.

Next day, in shocks of unbidden memory, a Budapest miracle all of Gabriel's own is announced. He is standing in Heroes' Square when for no reason a royal ghost, a prince of Siam on his way to Kiev, strides through him. And what's the rest of the story? Something dimly remembered about a girl. That's it, a girl from Kiev he marries, and she becomes his queen. Preposterous, yes, but not more so than most of what happens, and not only in Siam.

He sees by the *Herald-Tribune* that a former contract player at Warner Brothers and governor of California and pitchman for Arrow Shirts and Twenty-Mule-Team Borax has been elected president of the United States. Preposterous, yes. Also, that a supernova has occurred in the Large Magellanic Cloud, the galaxy next door to the Milky Way. Great creating nature sees to it that this happens from time to time. Well, what hasn't she seen to? A little after the moment of creation (of this particular universe anyhow), as the pure energy cooled, a slight disproportion of particles to antiparticles emerged. Were it not for that disproportion, antimatter would have cancelled out matter and closed the account and no universe would have come to be. If that original disproportion is not providential, Gabriel doesn't know what is. Such attunements are, in any case, providence enough for him. When Hubble showed a lady visitor from England his plates of galaxies millions of light years away, she gasped and said, "How terrifying!" Hubble said, "Only at first. Afterward, they give comfort. You know there's nothing to worry about. Nothing at all."

Two little memories smiting Gabriel Geismar: a Siamese prince and what Edwin Hubble said to Edith Sitwell. Two little stories held in counterpoise, one declaring that nothing is foreseeable, the other that everything is all right. You'd expect them, like the gingham dog and calico cat, to eat each other up. Instead, they are friends. Nothing's foreseeable, everything's all right: Somewhere between these two postulates is where always to be — in transit from the local to the cosmological and back again, by which trick of the mind you may know a brief but perfect freedom. This is how to live, Gabriel thinks. This is what to do.

Next day he flies from Budapest to Nice, drives from Nice to Orange, bicycles out from Orange, despite the autumn rawness, to a pretty house and garden in Sérignan du Comtat, barely noted in the guidebooks, with its lavender fields and olive groves, its eastern views to the Alps, its howling mistrals. In hermitage here, someone wise spent the last thirty years of life. Pass through a screen of sycamores and cypresses, down a lilac- and rose-bordered path to a wicker gate. You are upon sacred ground. When he cranks the bell handle the caretaker, roused from sleep, looks astonished, inclining Gabriel to wonder when the last visitor presented himself. *"Par ici aux merveilles du harmas. Le laboratoire, le jardin. Cent francs, si'il vous plait, monsieur,"* in heaviest Provençal accent.

Within, all is swept up, tidily bourgeois, solidly *dix-neuvieme*. First, the study: a tile floor, a walnut refectory table, an éscritoire no larger than a handkerchief, a globe. On a hook, J. Henri Fabre's linen jacket and broad-brimmed hat. Under a glass dome, his microscope. And in serried ranks on the shelves, the tens of thousands of entomological specimens. A stone martin, anciently preserved and mounted and running now to mange, rears and hisses from a high shelf.

Belongings may abide awhile with descendants — in attics, in basements, in glass-fronted cabinets. But then it's the landfill, the flea market, or the museum. Possibility number two is attractive: the flea market means one's things are getting a new lease. Really, though, it's purgatorial, it's what purgatory is, a going around and around. The true and only heaven of objects is museums, where they are charmed out of all further circulation. At this one, all is as Fabre left it when he died in the second year of the Great War, Fabre whose writ ran from the aftermath of Napoleon to the introduction of poison gas. He was a century. Look your fill around the place. When in fear, Gabriel nowadays tells himself just to look quietly at something, harder than he thought he could. A star. A bug. "Human knowledge will be erased from the world's archives before we possess the last word that a gnat has to say to us," wrote the very great man who trod these acres, the Shakespeare of the insects, gleeful, reverent, appalled, fond, incredulous, though never disapproving since these, his beloveds, are as incapable of wrongdoing as the stars. A book Gabriel had chanced to be reading the day his father died becomes at last holy writ, its burden a single mighty dictum encompassing stars and bugs, which is: metamorphosis, to change and change till you earn your death.

This garden, a laboratory of the open fields, was planted to lure all the insects of Europe: the pine processionary caterpillar, the long-horned green grasshopper, the Languedocian sphex, the bee-eating philanthus, the snail-shell bee. They have their instruction entirely from within, instinct making all they do predictable. Behold how the sacred beetle heaps up his ball of dung. Whereas we live by surprising ourselves and each other. With fullest force of purest instinct they know their tasks. We but guess at ours. They keep the terms of their contract. We negotiate as we go. They make their hives and hills. We make history.

Alone as Adam before Eve, Gabriel believes — against science — that the insects knew he was coming this afternoon, knew they had an appointment with him and kept it. Something makes the moment holy rather than intelligible. The glory of the world, hidden awhile, shows itself again. All is foreseeable, all is all right, unmathematizable mystery for which the pilgrim speaks today his thanks. *I am on my own but not alone*, he says to earth and air. *I'll expect nothing more.* There's loneliness in this but it's not altogether lonely. There's pain in this but it's not altogether painful. There's whistling in the dark in this, but it's not altogether scared. Here in this Eden, knowledge is not the opposite of innocence but its corollary. A contentment is provoked, a natural piety, by these things, stars, bugs, having nothing to do with us. How generous the arrangements are. Gabriel sinks down on hands and knees, the better to see a glowworm bathing in the dust, filmed over with it. She turns on her lamp. Look your fill, Geismar. Cheek to the ground. Get an eye even with her.